Pricey:

Playing in Traffic

Pricey:
Playing in Traffic

Fabiola Joseph

www.urbanbooks.net

Urban Books, LLC
300 Farmingdale Road, NY-Route 109
Farmingdale, NY 11735

Pricey: Playing in Traffic
Copyright © 2016 Fabiola Joseph

ISBN 13: 978-1-62286-519-2
ISBN 10: 1-62286-519-7

First Mass Market Printing July 2017
First Trade Paperback Printing September 2016
Printed in the United States of America

10 9 8 7 6 5 4 3 2 1

*This is a work of fiction. Any references or sim-
ilarities to actual events, real people, living or
dead, or to real locales are intended to give
the novel a sense of reality. Any similarity in
other names, characters, places, and incidents is
entirely coincidental.*

Distributed by Kensington Publishing Corp.
Submit orders to:
Customer Service
400 Hahn Road
Westminster, MD 21157-4627
Phone: 1-800-733-3000
Fax: 1-800-659-2436

Dedicated to Brandie Davis and Donnell White
Your love is inspirational.
It is proof that infinite love exists.
Thank you for allowing me to witness
something as beautiful
As the love that resides between the both of you.

The Law of Freedom

It is difficult to free fools from the
chains they revere.

—Voltaire

Acknowledgments

Brandie Davis, thank you for being a real friend. You are gifted, giving, strong, and at times, my sanity. You go far and beyond for not only me, but for everyone in your life. You are the best friend everyone deserves.

Papaya Wagstaff, you have been rocking with me since my first book. Thank you for being such a great friend. Thank you for all of your help. I needed someone like you. Luckily for me, I found you.

Qiana Drennen, I am so blessed to have you as a friend. Talk about selfless. You are the epitome of that word. You have a hard exterior, but on the inside, there's a beautiful heart and soul. You are one of the good ones.

Micole Walker, we may argue until the sun comes up, but I know you have my back. We fight like sisters, and although we don't speak as often as we used to, I respect and care for you very much.

TyKia Spencer, I love you, and I always will. I am so very blessed to have you in my life. I love you down to my soul, Boobie. Thank you for being you. You make my world a much more beautiful place. You are my rarest find. Most people only wish to find the beauty that is you.

N'TYSE, because of you I can walk into a store and see my books on the shelves. Thank you for making my dreams come true.

To my publisher, thank you will never be enough, but I offer it anyway.

My mother, who at heart's core is one of the most beautiful people I have ever known, I get my writing gift from you and the gods. Your poetry is the loveliest thing I have ever heard. When I was a kid, you used to perform around the Maryland area. I would just sit in the audience and be dazzled by your stage presence and words. You are beyond gifted, and even when you think nobody remembers or knows how much, I do and always will.

Brianna, looking at you, I see so much of me in you, and I just want to rescue you. I am your older sister, after all. Then the realest parts of you reappear and I smile. I know that you will be better than me, you will do more than me, and you will be everything you set out to be. You will be all that I regret that I am not, and that fills me with joy.

Chealsey, you inspire me with your strength and pure heart. Your health battles will never stop you, and I hope to one day have that kind of drive. We know exactly what the other is thinking with just one look. You are brave and beautiful, and I can't wait to see you on the big screen. You need to hurry up! Because of you, I will win my first Oscar for my movie script.

Granny Esperine, who I got all of this lip from (lol), there is not a stronger, more bullheaded, beautiful person on this earth who can fill your shoes. You're a tough cookie, but my God, what a woman. You are this family.

My supporters: There are no real words that will ever convey the happiness I feel and how thankful I am for my readers. I am different, I know. At times, I wonder if they ask themselves, "Where is this lady leading me?" I am out of the box, and my mind ranges from here to Timbuktu. I take you on a journey, and because of you, I do not travel alone. I have passengers with me who go through the same emotions as me. At times, I feel as if the people who read my work and truly understand it know me better than most in my life. You are friends who I don't have to know personally, friends that I don't have to speak to every day, but you are friends who are there for me. I appreciate you with every breath in my body. You are my invisible friends as I write, you are the reason I can call myself an author today. Yes, I was always a writer; that is the gift that was breathed into me by the gods, but because of you, I am an author.

Prologue

The Price of a Story

Her face was tight and shiny, showing the strain of previous plastic surgeries. I could tell that she was a little older than me. I was only twenty-five, and I wouldn't give her any older than her late twenties. We were a vast contrast against the other. While I dripped with diamonds and feminine wiles, she wore combat boots and had an air of misery about her. Although I suffered from a miserable past, I wore my pain on the inside, while hers was splattered across her face.

When I entered the pricey hotel room with Carmine and our entourage of protection, I wondered why it was so dark. It was midday, yet the room looked as if it was midnight. I got close enough to her, and knew instantly why she shied away from the light. Beneath her scars and anger, I could tell she was once a beautiful woman. Now I wasn't so sure how to feel about the woman who sat before me. The most attractive thing about her was her curly hair. Although at first glance you may have thought it wasn't combed, a longer glance would prove that theory wrong. Ringlets of curls fell in place, adding a touch of female wiles to her rough exterior as it danced against her brown skin.

In my short time here on this earth, I had met two people with the same names but spelled differently. Those two individuals would somehow forever change my life. Bobby Capello, the man who was responsible for the darkest period of my life; and this woman sitting right in front of me, whose name was Bobbi.

Carmine and I sat across from Bobbi. There were also three other men whom she brought to guard her. I was agitated from the second Carmine pushed this meeting on me. It wasn't that I knew the woman personally, but for some reason I just didn't like her. Two days before the meeting, Carmine called her without her being aware that she was on speakerphone. I started sensing something when Carmine informed her that he wanted to include me in their next meeting. She hastily questioned his decision to do so. I had to be involved and she didn't like that fact. *How dare this bitch? Maybe she didn't get the memo that Carmine never makes a move without me.*

I think what irritated me most was the fact that this was another female. We had it hard enough when it came to dealings in the underworld. Men looked down on us, considered us weak, and never treated us as equals. I fought my way to the top. I was forced to leave bodies, traitors, and even those I considered friends behind. Those sacrifices should earn respect and she was going to give me that. I was only twenty-five, but it seemed like I had lived a full lifetime. I had lost, taken, killed, and now I ruled. Even if she was to be forced to do so, she needed to respect me.

Our ill-tempered exchange of words and disrespectful glares had thickened the air to the point that I was taking in long, deep breaths. Her last comment about me being too young—as if Carmine wasn't just a few years older—touched a nerve. I looked at the lady who sat across from me and I turned my nose up in disgust. Not only did her outer appearance make her hard to look at due to all of the plastic surgeries, but her soul seemed to lack kindness.

"What in the hell do you know about me? Just because I am beautiful does not mean that my past was one of privilege. I had to fight to get to the top of the Pricey Pussy Empire just like you had to fight for your spot."

She laughed as I tried to stand up for myself. Her face was so tight and frozen that she no longer looked like a young woman in her late twenties. Instead, her smile only added falsely earned years to her expression.

"Carmine, this is why I told you I would rather just deal with you. Women bring along too much bullshit with them. Her attitude changed the minute she laid eyes on me."

Now it was my turn to laugh. I cocked my head back and bellowed out deep-rooted laughter, which I knew would anger her even more. "My attitude may have changed as soon as I laid eyes on you, but it doesn't have everything to do with what you look like. Beyond your face, your attitude is fucking disgusting; but I am quite curious. Tell me who, no, what are you? My God, what in the hell did you do to yourself? I am almost afraid to look at you. Not because you put any fear in my heart, but because I don't want to go home and have nightmares tonight."

What I said was unkind and evil and I wanted it to be. Resentment and pain flashed in her eyes and I knew I had her attention. Carmine reached over and, at first, tried to calm me down with a light pat on the knee. When he realized that his slight touch wouldn't work, he turned to me as if no one else was in the room. He lightly brushed my cheek with his hand and quickly kissed my lips. "Calm down, Billie Blue. Do this for me, my love. Calm down so we can talk."

Carmine was the only person who could douse my fire, and I was always the good angel on his shoulder. We understood each other's rage and could easily control the other's wrath.

With my feelings somewhat under control, I looked at the monster. What I found in her eyes took me back. In the place of resentment, I saw sadness. Bobbi's eyes were on Carmine's hand, which sat on top of mine. Instantly, I was able to relate to her for that brief moment. I took a few seconds to question the lack of love she may have been experiencing in her life. The look of longing swam steadily in her eyes against the strong current of loneliness that lingered in the vessels to her soul. But as quickly as it had appeared, the minute she raised her eyes to face me her moment of weakness disappeared.

"What have you ever had to fight for? First place in a beauty pageant? Life must have been so hard for you. But here is the thing: out there your looks matter, but in the world we have chosen to thrive in, your looks don't hold any weight. Well, not in mine at least. I sell drugs; I don't push cunt. There are a million cute bitches walking around L.A. I didn't question your looks because they matter. I am questioning your fucking guts. I want to know if you really have the balls to handle anything besides selling pussy."

I jumped to my feet and she was right behind me. There was no need to look around the room. I knew that my soldiers were just as ready as hers. I wasn't going to take too much of her disrespect without reaching out and showing her physically what I was all about. I had come a long way from that little girl who was taken from Haiti and placed in the Vega house. I was born from chaos and chose to continue on that path. It took me awhile to grow from meek and scared, and transform into a lioness who ruled her jungle while blood dripped from her fangs with pride. Now, I was a full-grown predator who would kill when provoked, and my claws were only seconds away from showing.

"It's not about my looks, huh? If that were really the case, why do they bother you so much? I came here to discuss business with who I thought was a businesswoman. Instead, you have chosen to wear your weaknesses on your sleeve. That anger and jealousy that is leaking from your pores isn't because you think that I am incapable of handling mine. No, that's not why. You didn't stand here throwing daggers at my beauty because you thought that it would stop us from making money. No, you just can't stand looking at what you will never be. We are two women who had to fight to stand in our positions; yet, just like a fucking woman, you would rather hate me for what I have, for what you lack, and for what you may never have again," I said, leaning into Carmine.

Bobbi stood in front of me, heaving for air. I watched as the beast damn near salivated at what I presumed was the thought of making me pay for my words. Her face was once again twisted with hate, but I was ready for whatever she wanted to do. I may have been selling sex and, to some, that was disgraceful. But, to me, respect needed to be shown no matter the game, because the players were all the same. No one was above the other. They came to me seeking pleasure from the sexiest men and women, and I supplied them with the best. As for her, she fed the dirty little drug habits of the people who yearned to escape the real world. From what I had heard, her shit was some of the best drugs around. Together, we were destroying the world in our own ways, so that made us even. We held keys that opened different doors, but those doors all led to the same destination: hell.

"Little girl, this game isn't for the beautifully weak. The pussy game doesn't hold a candle to the game I play. I can look at you and tell that you just don't have the heart."

At first, I wanted to rip her fucking tongue out of her mouth and force her to swallow it along with her words. She had no idea who she was speaking to. I took the Pricey Pussy Empire by storm and handled things as any man in power would. I also liked to think that I ran it better. To me, women had this elegance about them that men lacked. Even when I had to ruffle some feathers, no matter if it was a worker, a buyer, or a partner, I did it with grace and class. Carmine once told me that in the midst of fury, that was when I was the most beautiful. It didn't matter if I was being charming just to instill my will, or chopping off their goddamn heads, I did it the way only a woman could.

I stood there thinking about all of the grotesque ways I could make this old, bitter bitch suffer, but I knew that I could only fantasize about feeling the texture of her blood against my fingertips. Forcing her to show respect would do nothing but start a war, and I was much wiser than that.

"How about you sit the fuck down and let me tell you about who I am? I am asking nicely because if I opt to show you, you may not walk out of here alive," I said, still filled with anger.

Peering into my eyes, it was as if she saw something in them of interest. Her eyes softened and she backed away. Bobbi took her seat as she chuckled. She picked up her drink and crossed her legs. She played with her wild head of hair as if she was trying to get every strand into place; and, with a wave of the hand, she asked me to continue.

"Go ahead, Billie. Let's hear what brought your pretty little ass right in this room, at this very moment."

I looked at Carmine, and asked if he would fix me a drink. I took my seat, took a few deep breaths, and told her my story. No, I didn't just tell her my story; I told her our story. Bobbi sat and witnessed secondhand the evolution of Billie Blue Blondie and Carmine Pallazolo.

The Beginning

Planting the Seeds

Some are born this way
While others are
Forced to transform.

Chapter 1

The Price of Reality

There was that sound again, and it was making me crazy: "Get up you lazy bitch. Get up, Billie!"

The thin sheet was pulled off of me as I struggled to sit up. I was so tired. It seemed as if I had just gone to bed, yet there I was, getting up to start another dreadful day. Sitting up, I looked at Carmine. He always got up with me, no matter what. I guess you could say that we looked out for each other. Although our background stories were different, we were still living the same nightmare.

"Get up you stupid little bitch."

The slap across my face cleared the sleepiness from my body, and rocked me to my feet.

"I want you in that kitchen until I wake up."

Glancing at the dusty clock on the wall, I thought that my eyes were playing tricks on me. "It's only four in the morning. I don't have to get your breakfast ready for another three hours."

Instead of hitting me in the face again, Mrs. Vega pulled me close to her by my hair, and hit me twice in the head. Although she slapped me once before, she knew that she had to be careful. If her husband saw a bruise on me, the cruel hands of fate would turn the tables on her, and she would be the one on the receiving end of his violence.

"I don't give a shit what time it is. I want you in that kitchen and on your feet until I come down for my breakfast."

That time, I didn't answer. I had been through this before. Telling her that I had only had two hours of sleep would mean nothing to her. Mrs. Vega hated me, always had, and always would from what I could tell. She was just that type of woman.

Just the sight of Carmine reminded me of how ruthless Mrs. Vega could be. He was her nephew, yet she treated him like shit. She locked him in the basement with us, fed him scraps, and worked him as if he was a slave. Carmine was named after the Italian man his mother wished was his father. She even gave Carmine the man's last name. He came to live with his aunt after she promised his mother a better life for him. His journey to this hell hole was a long one. His boat trip from Cuba was rough, and it didn't match my entry into this country from Haiti. Late at night we would often sit up and talk about our past, as if reliving it would somehow give us an escape from the reality of our pitiful existence.

His mother was a whore in Cuba, but had managed to have two kids with just one man, Carmine Pallazolo. He had been his mother's regular customer for years, and they had two children together. Carmine's mother made a promise to Mr. Pallazolo years ago. She promised him that she would only have unprotected sex with him, and him only. So from then on, Mr. Pallazolo treated Carmelita, Carmine's mother, almost as a girlfriend. Sure, she continued being a whore, but Mr. Pallazolo treated her differently. He took care of all her bills, and took care of his children very well. He only allowed them to attend the finest schools. Pallazolo even got Carmelita to stop the sexual services she provided, but that wouldn't last too long. Carmelita harbored the scary thought that, one day, when Mr. Pallazolo was done with her, she would be left with nothing. So to ensure her family's future, she continued to sell her body, just not at the rate she was doing it before.

The breaking of Carmelita's promise to Mr. Pallazolo would have gone undetected if not for the birth of Carmine. His mother was a fair-skinned Cuban, and her two children before Carmine, twin girls, were birthed with white skin. Mr. Pallazolo's olive-colored skin dominated any melanin trait that may have lingered in the whore's bloodstream. The twins, Carletta and Marletta, were called *muchachas de la nieve,* meaning "snow girls," by the villagers because of their fair skin.

When Carmine was born the color of tar, his mother told him, her whole world changed. Mr. Pallazolo stopped coming around and she had to switch to turning tricks on a full-time basis. Carmelita told her son that she loved him, but there were times she just couldn't look at him. She begged Mr. Pallazolo to come back and see her from time to time, but he refused unless Carmine was no longer in the house. So, his mother called her sister, Mrs. Vega. She told her sister what happened and begged her sister to help. Mrs. Vega told Carmelita that her son would be better off in America, where he would go to the finest schools and, maybe someday, become a doctor. She fed her sister lies, and filled Carmelita's heart with dreams for her son that would never materialize.

Whenever Carmine would tell me about that boat trip to America, I would watch his face. His eyes would narrow as if the sound of his own words put him back on that little banana boat. As he spoke of the woman whose child would not stop crying, his whole body would shake. Carmine told me that the woman tried everything she could to quiet the sick child, but nothing would work. Finally, the man with the gun walked over to the lady and yanked the six-month-old child out of her hands. The woman jumped up and tussled with the man as much as she could but, soon, he would have the upper hand. The armed man held the woman down, then called Carmine over and gave him strict instructions: "Throw that baby off of the boat, or I'll throw the both of you off."

Carmine told me that he just stood there. He was all of eight years old and too young to understand the cruelty that the world housed, but old enough to know that he didn't want to get thrown off the boat.

"Do you hear me, little boy? Throw that damn baby off of this boat, or you will never make it to your aunt."

Carmine always seemed to get distant at this part. It was as if he had to step outside of himself not only when he picked up the baby, but also as he told me the story.

There he was, a sweet little boy at the tender age of eight, and he was forced to take a life. He told me that he had never heard such a sound. The mother's chilling call for help while her baby was in danger would forever be engraved in his mind. Rocking back and forth, Carmine relived his past through storytelling. He told me that he went numb as he picked the baby up by the arm. Carmine explained that he tried to make himself believe that the baby was just a rag doll, but the mother's shouting wouldn't let him escape.

"Please. Please, don't hurt my baby," she cried.

"Drop the fucking thing," the man ordered and watched as Carmine held the baby above the water. "You have one fucking second, or I'll let her go, and throw you over with the fucking brat."

Carmine closed his eyes and let the baby slide out of his hand. The man walked over to him after letting the mother go, and he patted him on the back. "This should teach you that life isn't really worth shit. One minute you're here, the next, splash, you're gone."

"But it was just a baby," Carmine said with tears in his eyes.

"A baby, a man, a woman; who gives a shit? Life is life and death is death. You killed to save your own, which is all that should matter to you."

Later that night as everyone tried to sleep, Carmine watched the baby's mother walk to the edge of the boat and look back at him. She looked him dead in his eyes, pointed, and wished him misery.

"They told me I would never have children but, by the grace of God, I did. Now you have taken from me what God has blessed me with. You have killed my miracle. For that, I pray that God makes you pay. And if He can't do it, may the devil hear my cries. May your life be filled with so much misery that you'll have no other choice but to take your own life, just as you have taken the life of my child. Do you hear me, Lucifer? I offer you this little black bastard. I offer you his soul," the mother howled to the dark sky.

With her words lingering in the night air, she jumped off the boat. Carmine was frozen with fear. With a gust of wind almost overturning the small boat, Carmine would often tell me, he could almost feel the devil's hand tugging at his feet.

Noticing Carmine's reaction to the mother's strong words, the man in charge laughed and said, "Thank God she jumped. My load is much lighter now."

That boat trip seemed to be haunting Carmine. Something in his eyes told me that he believed in the curse the woman wished on him. He believed that because of the curse, he was locked in

the basement with the rest of us. The only thing
that separated Carmine from the girls was that
his body wasn't being sold to the men, but to
the lonely women who came looking for a good
fuck. Mrs. Vega never did send him to school.
She kept him in the house and made him do odd
jobs like changing the sheets after the clients left,
and escorting them to the room when they first
arrived. The only time he got to dress up and feel
human was when he was working as her only
male whore. He slept in the basement with us.
That in itself was punishment enough.

The basement was a hellish place. Our mat-
tresses rested on cement floors. The walls were
a gray color, and I wasn't sure if it was paint
or filth. Chains hung from the walls and would
often be used to shackle us in place. When
Mr. Vega was home, the chains would only be
used on the person who stepped out of line. But
while he was gone, Mrs. Vega took pleasure in
"chaining the dogs," as she would say, referring
to us.

The smell wasn't always too pleasant either. If
a girl was sick and threw up or had an accident
on herself, we would have to sit with the odor
until Carmine had time to come clean it up.
After that, he was forced to report it to Mrs. Vega
and she would punish the girl by shackling her
in place and beating her, always making sure to
not leave visible marks.

There was a time when the one bathroom we shared got clogged up. Carmine reported it to his aunt but, since her husband wasn't home, she felt no real urgency to get it fixed. Day after day, we were forced to use the toilet and let the shit and urine build up. The stench was unbearable in the basement, but Mrs. Vega didn't care. We lived like pigs for a whole week before she had the toilet fixed, and that was only because Mr. Vega was due home the next day.

Carmine told me that when he first came to her home she made him strip. The minute she saw his penis she told him that, even at the young age of eight, he was too well hung to go to school. It was rare, but when women came to the house, Carmine would be gone for hours, sometimes days, and I always hated those times most of all. I was always afraid that Mrs. Vega would sell him off but, according to Carmine, Mrs. Vega told him he was too valuable. She told him that with his age and a dick like his, they would always have to come to her. So she kept him around. I guess that was why the other girls treated me so poorly. I had yet to be sold, and they all said that it was because Mr. Vega was in love with me. Whenever he was around, life wasn't as bad as it was when he went on trips for three and four days at a time.

When he was home, Mrs. Vega didn't mess with me much. I didn't have to do any housework or put up with her bullshit. I was able to shower and wear clean clothes. I would eat at the table with them, which allowed me to sneak Carmine big plates of food. I even got to sleep in one of the bedrooms upstairs, but that was the only part I halfway enjoyed.

Mr. Vega would come into the room and sleep with me. He would run his fingers through my hair, and tell me how beautiful I was. He would tell me that I could never celebrate my birthday because he wanted me to remain fifteen forever. Although Mr. Vega never penetrated me, he would do almost everything else.

He would spend hours licking my body from head to toe, and then he would take his time "pleasing" me orally. I had gotten used to returning the favor because he would ejaculate the minute my mouth touched his rod. He would then rub between my legs while whispering how much he loved me in my ear until he fell asleep.

He and Mrs. Vega would argue about me. Not because her husband spent his nights with me, but because she felt that it was time to sell me. Many men asked about me. Their customers paid top dollar for young girls, some coming from as far as Iran and Africa. Businessmen, kings, princes, and your average rich men frequented the Vega home in search of young, tender things. These powerful men would pay top dollar for a beautiful virgin like me. His wife spoke about it until she was almost blue in the face. Yet, her husband just couldn't sell me to the highest bidder. He once told me a bid went as high as five million.

"I am going back to bed. Get your ass in that shower and put these on," she said roughly, handing me one of the cute pink dresses and shoes Mr. Vega bought for me.

It had been three days since I was allowed to bathe and wear clean clothes. I think she did this as a way of putting me back in my place. The only bright side was that the clean garb meant that her husband would be coming home and her abuse would cease for a few days.

"After you're dressed, get your whore ass in that kitchen and stand in your corner until it's time to start breakfast."

When she walked away, I heard laughter coming from the three girls who hated me because Mr. Vega treated me nicely.

"Hurry up, bitch. You heard her. Get your whore ass clean and in that kitchen," the ringleader said. She was the worst of them all. Erin, a beautiful black American girl with scars across her face and all over her body, hated me from the minute she saw me. Hell, it seemed as if she hated the whole damn world. Once Carmine told me what happened to her face, I understood her rage.

The Vegas had a client from the Middle East with very specific needs. He wanted a beautiful black girl who he could cut and scar at his whim. At times, he would come into the country, have sex with Erin, and not hurt her. Then, there were the dark times that she would leave the basement and not come back for days. When she did return, she would be bandaged from head to toe.

A few weeks later, after the bandages came off, she would have a new scar, physically and mentally. It seemed as if with every new slash she acquired across her skin she would become meaner. We all knew what was going on but we never brought it up. Ignoring her was the best thing for her. The hell she was living was something that I would never understand, so I considered her attitude appropriate for her circumstances.

Chapter 2

The Price of Pussy

Carmine and I stood in the corner of the kitchen as instructed. The other girls were shackled one floor below us. Carmine and I made small talk. He kept me company until five minutes before Mrs. Vega's normal breakfast hour.

When her husband was home, the cook made breakfast, but while he was gone, she told the maid and cook to take a load off, then made me do all of the work. Her breakfast consisted of eggs, bacon, fruit, bagels, and a variety of jams. Accompanying that was coffee, and a mimosa. While Mrs. Vega feasted on a meal fit for a queen, I sent the girls their normal breakfast: oatmeal, one slice of wheat toast with no butter, and a small box of apple juice. Mrs. Vega weighed us girls once a week. If any of us were over 130 pounds, she would make the "fat pig" skip a meal or two until the following week. I made a plate for Carmine from Mrs. Vega's rations and sent him downstairs.

While I was serving the food, the real cook came walking into the kitchen and announced that Mr. Vega was pulling up. His wife looked at me, and instructed me to sit down at the table and put food on my plate.

I rolled my eyes at how fake she was, and I plopped down on the chair beside her. In some sick way, I was actually excited that Mr. Vega was home. Sure, things were better when he was there but, deep down inside, I knew that it was much more than that. A part of me had fallen for him. I guess I didn't know any better. Later on, I found out about Stockholm syndrome, and chalked it up to that. It was weird though. Whenever he left, sadness would come over me. Then, when he would return, I would get butterflies and a slight happiness would set in.

Sitting at the table with my untouched food in front of me, I watched the door like a dog waiting for her owner. The moment I heard the door open, the sound of his footsteps helped widen my smile.

"Wipe that fucking smile off of your face. That is my husband," Mrs. Vega whispered, but I paid her no mind.

"Hello, beautiful. I hope that you were okay while I was gone." Mr. Vega bypassed his wife and greeted me first. The smell of his cologne sent chills down my spine as he stood me up and gave me a hug.

Mrs. Vega slammed her coffee mug down, causing it to shatter. Her husband turned to her and placed his hand on her shoulder. "Hello, Elena. How are you?"

I watched the muscles in Mrs. Vega's jaw tighten as she gave her husband a cold glance. Then she shrugged, and said, "Fine."

Later, I had fallen asleep on the comfortable bed when a shouting match between Mr. Vega and his wife woke me up.

"She must do it. It is time. She is in her prime and seven million dollars is record-breaking!"

"He isn't asking to just sleep with her. He wants to take her away. He wants to buy her!"

"Who gives a shit? She's just another whore. I'm sorry but it has already been done. He deposited his money this morning."

"What? What do you mean it is already done?"

"I sold your little bitch, that's what. I hate that girl and I can't wait to see her go!"

The couple continued to argue as the blows her husband punished her with echoed through the house. I got out of the bed and tiptoed to the door.

"Marco!" Mr. Vega yelled after dealing with his wife. "Get Capello on the phone. I need to stop a sale."

I pressed my ear to the door and tried my best to hear what would be, to me, a one-sided conversation. My heart raced because something was telling me that Mrs. Vega was talking about me when she said she sold his bitch. Although I should have listened to my gut feeling, I forced myself to believe that I was wrong. I prayed she didn't have the power to go over her husband's head and make a deal.

While Mr. Vega argued with who I presumed was Capello on the other end of the phone, Mrs. Vega's backtalk lessened. Soon, all I could hear was her laughter from time to time. Once the ruckus died down, I got back in bed and dozed off again, only to be awakened by Mr. Vega's warm body.

Something about Mr. Vega was off that day. He touched me, but it was with more passion. His kisses were longer, and his tongue moved slowly as if he was taking the time to savor my flavor.

"I love you, Billie."

His whisper lingered in the air while his tongue fought to bring me to climax. I was never able to have an orgasm with him, no matter how hard he tried. He would nurse my clit for hours trying to teach me how to have an orgasm, but it just wouldn't happen. The things he did felt good but they never worked. That day with him was the closest I had ever come but, still, no cigar.

"Billie, I have something that I need to tell you," he said, coming up from between my thighs. Lying next to me, he licked and dined on my nipples between his words.

"Tell me, *papi*."

My eyes were closed as I listened to his smacking lips against my perky breasts. I lay beside him peacefully and waited for an answer. When I didn't feel his lips any longer or hear a response, I opened my eyes and looked at him.

Mr. Vega appeared to be in misery as he looked down at me. I prayed that what I was thinking was wrong. "Tell me, *papi*. Come on, tell me."

I moved even closer to him. With my skin against his, I reached down and found his dick. I massaged it, and added a kiss. I hoped to assure him that I was his and that he could tell me anything. He kissed me back and once his hand found my moist sweet spot, he stopped kissing me. I opened my legs wider just how he liked it. He loved looking at me down there. He always told me that it was the prettiest thing he had ever seen, besides my face.

"I love you so much, *papi*. You make me feel so good."

I knew he liked to hear those words but instead of him smiling like he usually did, he started to cry. His hands stopped moving. Then, resting his head on my chest, he just cried.

"What is it, *papi?* Please, just tell me."

"I'm so sorry, Billie. I really am sorry."

"What is it, *papi?* Tell me."

"Elena has sold you."

After his words hit me, the room seemed to start spinning. I sat up, holding my head, and said, "What do you mean she sold me? You told me that I belonged to you. You told me that she would never be able to do that."

With tears still running down his face, Mr. Vega came over to my side of the bed and sat beside me. "I tried to stop the sale. I even called our boss, Capello. I spent three hours making calls and even offered to return the man's money. But, there is no going back once a sale has been done."

I wanted to cry and scream, but my tears just wouldn't fall. Instead, I was flooded with resentment. I envisioned myself with a knife in my hand running around the house, and cutting the heads off of everyone in there except for Carmine.

"I fucking hate you! You didn't try hard enough. All this time you were telling me that you loved me, but you really don't. You just care about money." I knew that my words would cut deep into his emotions and, in that moment, I wanted to shred them.

"That is not true at all, Billie. Trust me, I tried everything that I could."

He was trying to wrap his arms around me, but I pushed him away and got off of the bed. His wife stormed into my bedroom. She had never done this before. Her lip was busted, and both of her eyes were puffy.

"That's right, bitch. I sold your ass. Today will be the last time you ever have my husband in your bed."

I didn't answer right away. By the time I went to open my mouth, Mr. Vega tackled his wife, causing her to fall. He kicked her head viciously before dragging her out of the room by her hair. She cried out and tried to grab anything that could stop her exit. Any time she'd latch on to a piece of furniture, Mr. Vega would stomp on her hands until she'd let go.

Chapter 3

The Price of Truth

I sat in the room for an hour without moving or saying a word. Mr. Vega returned to the room only to find that I had locked the door. He pleaded with me to open it, but I told him that he needed to give me some alone time. I heard a knock at the door again, and I assumed that it was him.

"Just give me a little more time," I answered, not wanting to be bothered with Mr. Vega.

"It's me, Billie."

Hearing Carmine's voice was the medicine my soul needed. Rushing to the door, I pulled him into the bedroom and hugged him tightly. I waited for him to do the same. Then I felt his arms around my waist, and felt safe enough to talk.

"Mrs. Vega sold me, Carmine. What am I going to do?"

He was quiet and didn't say a single word. I let go of him so I could see his face. For the first time since knowing Carmine, I was scared of him. The look in his eyes was easy to read. I was almost sure that Carmine was seeing red.

"Carmine, what am I going to do? I can't leave here, nor can I leave you. I just can't!"

I watched him walk over to the chair that I was sitting in previously, and he just stared off into space. "So she is just going to sell you off as if you're cattle?"

As much as I hated to admit it, I was no more important to Mr. Vega then the other girls. "Yes, just like the ones before me, Carmine, and I'm sure just like the ones who will come after me."

Again, Carmine's response was one of deep silence. Finally, looking at me, he said, "Let's kill them. If we get rid of them, they won't be able to sell you off."

I watched Carmine, forcing myself to believe that he was talking out of his ass. Just hours before this, I envisioned myself hacking the heads off of everyone who had a hand in this, but it was not reality. "As much as I would love to do that, it will just have to stay in my fantasies for now."

"Why?"

"Why what?" I asked Carmine.

"Why can't we kill them? They are horrible people. No one will miss them."

I stood there envisioning the satisfaction that I would feel as Mr. and Mrs. Vega would take their last breath; but I wasn't a killer. So, I stood in that room in complete silence, and devised a plan.

"Carmine, do you trust—"

"Yes," he answered before I could even finish my sentence.

I took his hand and asked him to follow me.

"Where are we—"

I shushed him and walked him to the bed. Then I said, "Carmine, I don't want to be sold off like a piece of meat."

"I don't want that to happen either," he answered in his fleeting Cuban accent.

"I need you to take from me what they want the most."

He stood there as if he didn't have the faintest idea what I spoke of. I patted the bed and waited for him to sit beside me. I took his hand and didn't waste any time. "I need you to have sex with me."

He was quiet, and I tried to read his mind. He wouldn't look at me as he spoke, and his hand started to sweat. "Billie, we . . . I . . . We . . . Maybe that's not the right thing to do. How will that help you?"

I got off of the bed, kneeling before him so that I could look into Carmine's eyes. I said, "That's what they want from me: my virginity. I was once told that because I am beautiful and untouched, I was worth a lot of money. Maybe if my virginity is no longer on the table, the buyer will want his money back."

"I don't know, Billie. What if—"

"Look, Carmine, I need you to do this for me. Please, please, Carmine. This is my only hope."

I went to the door, locked it, and went back over to him. Wrapping my arms around his neck, I kissed Carmine's lips for the first time. Kissing him felt different from what I felt when Mr. Vega's lips were on mine. I was only fifteen and Carmine, seventeen. Our kiss just felt right. We had always had this chemistry, and there was an electrical charge pulling us together.

He was a caregiver. Someone who I knew would always be there for me. There was no reason; I just felt it. So when he kissed me back, things began falling into place. Pulling away from his lips, I stood in front of Carmine. His eyes followed my hands as they pulled at my clothes, disrobing me.

My young body kissed the air as I took a few steps forward, and got closer to him. Carmine's hands ran up my thighs, up my backside, and ran over my waist. I leaned into him, letting my nipple touch his lips. I moaned as they parted and I felt his tongue wet it.

"Yes, Carmine, that's it. You know, I have never gone all the way. You are going to have to teach me."

"How do you want me to do it? You want it fast, you want it slow? They usually tell me."

I cupped his face in my hands and kissed him before I said, "I don't want you to fuck me like those old bitches. I want you to make love to me, Carmine. Let this flow, and make me feel good. Feel my body, and let me feel yours."

There was no need to say anything else. Carmine stood up, picked me up, and we got in the bed. Carmine felt different from the only other man who had ever touched me. He kissed and licked every part of my body and, for the first time, it was on fire. My frame was engulfed in the flames of passion. I tried to control my moaning, but eventually he just had to put the pillow over my face. Carmine was as skilled as I imagined he would be. He often told me about the woman Mrs. Vega had brought in to teach him about pleasing a woman. From what I could tell, she taught him well.

"Come on, Carmine. We don't have much time. Let me feel you."

Although I did love everything that he was doing to me, time was of the essence. Feeling his hot pipe against my thigh, I looked down at it, and saw that it was engorged with blood, long, big, and black. For a second, I asked myself if I was really ready, but I quickly reminded myself that I had no choice. As Carmine rubbed his pole against my clit, I opened my legs wide, waiting for him to slide in.

"Before I do it, I must tell you something," he said.

I stayed quiet with the pillow still over my face. My body fought my mind as the wetness between my legs invited him in. In my mind, I was screaming, *I am so fucking nervous,* and I hoped Carmine's words would soothe my nerves.

"I have always thought about this. I have always wanted to make love to you. And I have always loved you from the minute you walked through that door. I have always loved you."

I removed the pillow from my face and just stared at him.

Carmine pushed his way into my body. Our eyes were locked on each other. Biting into my bottom lip, I felt him work his way into my cave.

First came the pain. It was almost as if I could hear my body stretching to accommodate him.

Then, he began rubbing my clit, and his dick sliding in and out of me became pleasurable. My hands found his ass, and I pulled him deeper into me. It was as if our bodies were one. We were so in tune, and had channeled the one thing that bonded us together. That was the love we had for each other.

His mouth muffled the sounds of ecstasy leaving my body as I orgasmed. I exploded with him inside of me. In that moment, I understood why Mr. Vega had tried so hard to get me to do it with him. Carmine was my first. I experienced my first orgasm with him, and we would always have a bond. When my body yearned for the touch of a man, he would be the first person to cross my mind. When a man entered my body, I would close my eyes and see him.

My God, did he make me feel good. Even after my very first orgasm, he kept on going. He made sweet love to me the first time around. Then, for the second round, he fucked me so damn good. He moved his hips to what seemed to be a warrior's rhythm. He sucked and licked on my nipples as his sweet meat filled me up, and left me satisfied. He whispered my name, telling me that he loved me with such thirst and hunger that all I wanted to do was give him more of me. We fucked like animals. Lunging and pulling at each other's bodies, we acted as if this would be the last time we indulged in such a feast. We exploded together, and I told him that I loved him too, and that I always would.

When we were done, I spent ten minutes lying in his arms with no words spoken. I pretended that I was not in the Vega household, but in our own house, and in our own bed. After, I told him to get dressed, and I watched him do so. The wetness between my legs and his scent left imprints of him in my brain.

"Are you going to get dressed?" he asked as he headed for the door.

"No, because if I do it will be as if this never happened."

He looked back at me and I saw it in his eyes. He walked over to me and, while still standing, he leaned down and kissed me. After, as he cupped my breast and ran his thumb across my nipple, he said the truest words that I had ever heard.

"Billie Blue, nothing in this world can take away what we did, or what we have. It happened, and I will kill before I let anyone take you away from me."

Chapter 4

The Price of Our Past

I did not get out of that bed until Mr. Vega came back to the room. He cried some more, which had no effect on me. After what Carmine and I shared, the feelings that I once had for Mr. Vega were gone, and it was as if they never existed at all. He even tried to touch me, but I wouldn't give him the satisfaction of copping one last feel. I laughed inside as I thought of the plans I had for that night. When his wife came barging into the room again, she said that it was time.

"Time for what?" her husband asked.

"She needs to get ready. Her buyer will be here in two hours."

Mr. Vega left the room without even taking a second look at me.

"Get up, go downstairs, and get a box from Carmine. Get your things from the basement and everything from this room. I can't wait to watch you walk out of this house. I should have known that you would be a curse. No poor black girl should have been blessed with those blue eyes. I hate you, and I hope that your buyer is an evil one. I hope that he does things to you that will leave you dead in the end."

Mrs. Vega stood at the foot of the bed I was lying in. I watched her eyelids lower into small slits. The smoke from her cigarette swam in the air. I was guessing that she was waiting for a nasty reaction from me; instead, I smiled and got out of the bed, making sure to cover the small spot of blood left behind from my broken hymen. I walked over to her as naked as the day that I was born. Then I stood in front of her and tried my hardest to cripple her tainted soul with my words.

"The hatred that you have in your heart for me, when did it form? Did it start to grow the minute you and your husband found me in the open market with my mother? Did that seed plant itself when you noticed how your sick husband lusted over my thirteen-year-old body? Or did it start to grow when you realized that your husband loved coming into my room at night just so he could suck on my sweet, young pussy?"

Reaching down between my legs, I ran my fingers between the lips of my vagina. My fingers came back up wet from the delicious juices my body created with Carmine just a few moments earlier. Rubbing my fingers across the top of her lips, I continued to spit the poison that would kill her dying soul for good.

"You smell that? Do you feel that wetness? Well, that is what your husband loves about me the most."

Pulling away from me, Mrs. Vega wiped off her top lip. Then she glared at me, but I was ready for her.

"Don't even bother. That smell, that texture, I'm sure it will forever be embedded in your mind. Your husband has a way of making me so wet when he touches me. See, what you need to understand is he loves me, he wants me, and I make him cum, not you!"

Mrs. Vega suddenly charged at me and, as she had done on many other occasions, she raised her hand to slap me. But this time, as her hand came down, I caught it. Then I said, "You do not get to hit me anymore. I am no longer yours, remember?"

Mrs. Vega raised her left hand in an attempt to try to strike me again. This time, I held on to both of her hands. Then I got so close to her that I could smell the liquor on her breath.

"You took me from my mother, from my country, and you brought me into your home. You lied to the only woman I have ever loved, and you let your husband come into my bed and lick, suck, and touch me all over my body. I am not a curse but you, bitch, you fucked yourself the day you brought me here. So you smell this. You remember the scent of little Billie Blue Blondie. Memorize it, and know that this is the one little girl you just could not break."

Letting go of one of her hands, I rubbed my fingers across her top lip again before continuing. "You remember that smell every time you think of that cold, empty space in your bed. You think of it and picture your husband touching me and telling me that he loves me. As we both know, he sure as hell doesn't love you. And the more I think about it, maybe that's why you're so damn evil," I spat then watched for her reaction.

The look on that rotten old bitch's face went from anger to surprise. She seemed to doubt herself and turned away to hide how uncomfortable she was with her uncertainty, but I caught it. I enjoyed the smell of doubt and defeat that loomed in the air.

For the first time since meeting Mrs. Vega, I saw the real her. She was a sad old bitch who thrived on the fear she instilled in the little girls she stole. She was really powerless, and she only felt mighty when she stood over the young girls she tried to break.

Walking over to the bed, I pulled off the sheet as I hummed a melody that I made up. From the corner of my eye, I watched the wretched, coldhearted woman, and she had not moved. I walked out of the room with the sheets in my hand, still naked. I didn't bother to get dressed as I made my way to the basement to get the box from Carmine and give him the sheets to store in a safe place until I needed them.

I didn't want to shower and get all dressed up for my buyer, but in order for my plan to work I had to. So as I put my belongings from the basement in the box, Erin's nosey ass must have sensed that something was different.

"Where in the hell are you going? Moving upstairs for good?" Erin asked.

Even though I wasn't happy, I smiled at her. I knew that Erin had been deemed unsellable, unless the customer who liked to come over and cut her wanted to put up the cash. In a sick way, I think that fact bothered her.

"No. I was just sold to a prince," I lied.

The smirk was wiped clear off her face. "What? What do you mean? They can't sell you. It should be me. It should be me," she said more to herself, but we all heard it.

I got in her face, smiled, and said, "Well, it ain't you. Never will be you, either. No one wants a scarred-up, ugly bitch like you."

Erin charged me and we both fell to the floor as she said, "Scarred? Scarred? I'll show you scarred. Sofia, hand me that razor."

Erin was on top of me. She was heavy and no matter how hard I tried to push her off, I just couldn't do it. After Sofia handed Erin the razor, her hand came down fast, just not fast enough. I knew that she cut me. I just wasn't sure how long or how deep. I thanked God for Carmine because he yanked her off of me and punched her dead in the face, knocking her out.

"Oh my God. Carmine, I'm bleeding," I said as I looked at my shoulder.

"It's small. Let's clean it up," Carmine said in a reassuring tone.

The cut wasn't that bad, half an inch across my shoulder. Carmine shackled all of the girls to the walls. I took one last look around the basement, and vowed never to step foot in it again . . . unless it was to get even.

I watched the clock and, with each second that passed, I wondered how my night would play out. There were only twenty minutes left on the clock before my buyer was set to arrive. My knees were shaking. Carmine was all dressed in his tux with white gloves to boot. That was one thing that I had to hand to the Vegas: they tried to run their seedy business with class.

"Are you ready for this?" Carmine whispered.

"Well, as my mother would say, you never know what you're ready for unless you have no choice but to face it head-on."

Thoughts of my mother filled my mind at the oddest moments. The night Mr. Vega told me the value I had on my head, I was in his arms, and I thought about my past life and the one that I was living in that moment. Nestled in the arms of the man who thought that sexually violating me was love, I also thought about my mother. The only thing I had left connecting me to her was the picture that was in the gold locket Mr. Vega gave me.

Every night I thought about her, and every night I wondered if she was worried about me. The day I left Haiti was the last time I had ever spoken to her. My mother was the greatest woman I had ever known, and she loved me even though I was conceived in chaos.

My mother was birthed from hardworking parents. They had very little and worked from dusk 'til dawn to feed their small family. Waking up at four in the morning, they'd walk four, five hours to go sell their vegetables at the market-place. My mother never went to school because her parents just didn't have the money, but one thing she always had was beauty. At the age of thirteen, she stood five feet ten inches. Although she didn't have a lot of luxuries, the one thing she always did was dye her hair blond.

One of the white boys who lived in the big house down the road once told her that her last name, Blondie, meant someone with blond hair. From that day on, she wanted her features to match the unique name. The hair color made her stand out, and added to her physical charm.

By my mother's fourteenth birthday, my grandmother had fallen ill and could no longer go to the market. Soon, her father had to stay behind to tend to her mother, Carmell. The sweet sounds of Billie Holiday kept my mother company on those long walks to the market, as the family's bills now rested on her back with one sick parent and one playing nurse.

One early morning, as my mother set out on that long walk with pride, the cruel hand of fate would rest its fingers right between her legs. My mother, Betty, was never really too clear with me about what happened, but the one thing I knew for sure was that I was the product of rape.

Four men raped her at the tender age of fourteen; three were white, and one was black. By the time she got back home and told her father what happened, she found out that her mother was dead. Drowning in grief and anger, her father didn't believe that she was raped. So she found herself on the streets alone, and pregnant with a child who was fatherless. She did odd jobs, but once her stomach got too big, work was hard to find. Even in the city of Port-au-Prince, no one wanted a teenager they thought was hot in the pants.

When I was born, my mother said that her luck changed; everyone wanted the little Haitian baby with the blue eyes around. She was even able to land a job as a maid for a lady who never had children and lived alone. But once the woman started to think that I was her child, my mother left the job and found herself selling coal on the streets. We didn't have much, but being with my mother was heaven, even if it was in a tin house with no running water or electricity.

Selling coal on the streets of Haiti was how I met Mr. Vega. As I went to get lunch from the street vender, he walked up and offered to buy the food. I turned him down and hurried back to my mother with him following. The first day, he spoke to my mother and told her how beautiful

I was. He came around for a week straight, and on the eighth day, his wife showed up with him.

"What is her name?" the beautiful lady with the flowing dress asked.

"Billie Blue," my mother answered with a smile.

"Is her last name Blue?" the man asked.

"No, that is her name: Billie Blue. Her last name is Blondie," my mother said with pride as she stroked her own blond hair.

"Your daughter is very beautiful. She could go to America and become a model. That will make her rich," Mrs. Vega told my mother.

At first, my mother was against letting me go to a new country without her, but the Vegas were persistent. For a whole month they beat my mother down with visions of her daughter becoming a famous model. They brought what I now know were fake photos of girls they said now lived in Paris and London. The Vegas told my mother that the girls worked for their modeling agency and graced the covers of magazines, and how some even acted on television. Finally, after renting a small apartment for my mother, taking her out, and even taking us shopping for clothes, my mother gave in. The last time I hugged my mother was February fourteenth, my thirteenth birthday.

Chapter 5

The Price of Betrayal

"Billie. Billie Blue, your new life is here. Get up and greet the man."

I was so far into my thoughts that I hadn't even noticed the man standing in front of me. When I looked up, I stopped breathing. He was a fat white man who was licking his lips as he looked me over.

"My God. I have always seen her walking around, but up close she's even more beautiful than I thought."

"Say hello, Billie."

I walked up to the man and shook his hand without saying anything.

"Carmine, take them to the newlywed room."

My stomach dropped. The fat man was breathing heavily while climbing the steps behind me. Once at the bedroom door, Carmine whispered that the bloody sheets were in the closet.

***

We had been sitting in the room for ten minutes, with me on one side of it, and him on the other.

"Come and sit with me," the white man said, patting the mattress.

I walked over to him and sat on the bed, and his hand quickly began crawling up my thigh.

"You are so beautiful, and that hair, that long hair is so beautiful." He ran his hand through my mane while sliding his other hand farther up my thigh. It made me nervous, but I had other thoughts on my mind.

"Why did you buy me?" I asked.

The white man seemed amused as he looked at me. "Because I can. I am a collector of fine things and I am adding you to my collection."

I felt sick to my stomach, but asked, "What about your wife or children? Do you have any?"

"My wife and kids will never know of you. I have a very nice house that I set up for you. You will want for nothing as long as you give me what I want."

I didn't have to ask about what he wanted because his hand slid up my skirt, parted my legs, and he began to rub my clit from the outside of my panties.

"Where is this house, and how do you know that I won't run away?" I asked.

The fat man laughed until he turned red. Then he said, "You will not run away because I will kill you. Well, I should say, have you killed. You won't be there alone. I have hired two men to keep you in check. Plus, I always get what I want. When I see something that grabs my interest, such as you, I do what I can to get it."

"Where is this house?" I asked.

"California. I have a beautiful home there, just like this one. Aren't you tired of living down South? There's so much to do out West. You'll love it."

I didn't answer but I did have more questions. So I asked, "But why me? There are other girls here."

His hand worked its way from the outside of my panties. Now he was feeling around on the inside. My body jerked once he touched my bare skin.

"I have been with other girls here, but none as beautiful as you. You're different. You don't walk around like you're broken. When I found out that you were untouched and hard to buy, I just knew you were the one."

I looked at him and knew that the time had come. "I am not untouched."

When I said it, my voice did not waver. I was straight forward, forceful even.

"I know, honey, because I am touching you now," he said as he leaned into my neck and kissed it.

"No, that is not what I mean," I said as I spread my legs and took control of his hand that was between them.

"See, before you came today, I got fucked by a big black dick. Go ahead, slide your finger in and feel what I am telling you," I said with a slight grin.

Then I waited and watched his jaw drop at what I instructed him to do. He shook his head in disbelief. So I held his middle finger, inserted it inside of me, and slid up and down. Looking in his eyes, I saw the pleasure from the sexual exchange, and pain, as the truth dawned on him.

"You feel that? That's no virgin pussy. That is the wetness of a girl who knows what it's like to have a good, big, black dick inside her. Hell, even Mr. Vega knows what this pussy feels like. He's been playing in it since the minute I walked into this house."

Now I could see his fat face swelling with disgust. He yanked his hand from between my legs. Then, pushing me off of the bed, he started calling for Mrs. Vega. "Get in here quickly!"

The hateful woman came running into the room with a puzzled look on her face. Glancing

at me then him, she asked, "What's wrong?
What's going on in here?"

"You sold me used goods. How could you lie to
me and take my money?" the angry white man
growled.

"What . . . what are you talking about? Surely
this is a misunderstanding," Mrs. Vega said with
a halfhearted smile.

"She is not pure. And to think she had a black
man inside of her just today. I am so disgusted. I
want my money back."

Turning to me, Mrs. Vega gave me the evil eye.
Her tone was laced with anger when she asked,
"What is he talking about, Billie? You better tell
him that you are lying right now!"

Without answering her, I walked to the closet,
and pulled out the sheets. Then I held on to one
end and threw the other half with the dark red
bloodstain over the bed. The evidence of my
impurity was smack dab in front of them.

"No lies in here. Except for the one you told
this man about me being untouched." I smiled,
amused. I watched both of them glancing down
at the bed then back at me in disbelief. Shock
filled the room, but I was grinning from ear to
ear.

"You told me if I did what you wanted, I could
have her. I not only killed her mother, but I also
paid cold, hard cash for, what, a lie?"

The white man went on talking, but I didn't want to hear the rest of it, so I interrupted and asked, "Wait, sir, what do you mean, 'killed her mother'?"

He didn't answer me, but that evil bitch Mrs. Vega finally spoke up. "Just a going-away present, honey. That bitch mother of yours is dead. Now, how does it feel? You thought that you had the upper hand, didn't you? Now look at you, mouth hanging all open." She chuckled.

I charged Mrs. Vega and tried my best to kill her. My mother? How could she have my mother killed? I could feel the white man tugging at me from behind as I fought the bitch. He pulled me off of her and, as he held me down, Mrs. Vega started to slap and punch me. Blow after blow, she laughed and told me the fat man told her how my mother cried and pleaded for her life. I was sure that she would have killed me if it weren't for Carmine. He came running into the room with an ax, and with one heavy swing the white man's head went flying off of his shoulders.

The room went still and it gave me a moment to take everything in. I stood up beside Carmine and went blank. Mrs. Vega's voice was what brought me back. She screamed for her husband and, as Mr. Vega came rushing in, Carmine swung the ax at his leg, hacking into the left one.

As Mr. Vega fell, Carmine dragged him into the room and I locked the door behind them.

"She killed my mother, Carmine. She killed my mother," I wept.

I was leaning into him and buried my face in his shoulder as I cried for my mother. Carmine pushed me away and headed toward Mrs. Vega.

"Don't do this, Carmine. I am your aunt, your family," Mrs. Vega pleaded.

She fell to her knees and locked her fingers in the air as if she was about to say a prayer, but God would turn a deaf ear that night.

"She's right, Carmine. Let me."

I walked over to him and took the ax from his hand.

"Just tell me why. Why would you kill my mother on top of what you have already done to me?"

That filthy animal looked right into my eyes and I'm guessing decided to die with all of the resentment she felt toward me still in her heart.

"Because I fucking hate you, that's why. When I thought about things, I knew that before you left this house, I needed you to feel the same pain that I had felt time and time again as my husband left my bed for yours. That's right, I did it because I fucking hate—"

I picked up the ax and hacked at her head until pieces of it were missing. Mr. Vega's cries fell on deaf ears because, from that very moment, I would never be the same. I knew that as Mrs. Vega's soul left her body, mine followed soon after.

Chapter 6

The Price of Our Sins

"What about him?" Carmine asked.

There was a feeling of sympathy growing inside me when I glanced at Mr. Vega. There lay the man who would sneak into my room and feel me up yet, somehow, he kept me sane. He was the only one besides Carmine to ever show me some type of love while I was stuck in that house.

I walked over to him and looked at his bleeding leg. He looked up at me with fear in his eyes and, for the first time that day, I felt as if I was in total control.

"Did you know about my mother?"

"No, Billie, I swear I didn't. I would have never allowed it. Please don't kill me, Billie. I love you. I really didn't know about your mom."

I stood there looking down at him and felt pity. I asked Carmine to sit him up and tie his hands to the foot of the bed.

"I love you, Billie. Please, don't kill me."

I stood in the middle of the room and took off all of my clothes. I asked Carmine to get a pen and a paper and asked him to take notes.

"If you love me, tell me how all of this is run. I want to know the ins and outs of your underground corporation."

"Why? Why do you need to know that?"

"Because, I want to take your wife's place. Now that she's gone, I can become yours, and we can take over the world with this business."

Mr. Vega smiled and ran off names and what positions they held. He gave me addresses and phone numbers. He also told me who was at the top of the totem pole, as far as the human trafficking ring. Capello was the boss, and I knew that he was the man I needed to get in contact with. When he was done and it all had been written down, I walked over to Mr. Vega and stood in front of him.

"Now, I want you to make me cum."

The smile that spread across Mr. Vega's face let me know how sick of a man he really was. There he was, tied up and minutes away from death, but the thought of touching me blinded him to those facts.

His back was against the bed, so I told him to lean his head back as I squatted over his face. I wanted to see if in his dying moment he could make me cum. It was twisted, it was almost demonic, and it turned me on. As I inched closer to the dark side, I motioned for Carmine to get behind Mr. Vega.

"Oh, shit, you did it, you did it. I'm about to cum."

Mr. Vega sucked on my clit hungrily. He worked harder than he ever did to achieve what he had been after for so long. I had an orgasm like no other and, as I pulled away from Mr. Vega, I noticed the smile on his face.

"You did it, *papi,* you did it."

"I always knew I could," he answered.

I turned my back on him, got dressed, and made my way to the bedroom door. "Look up," I told him with my back still to him.

"No, no, no, please, Billie. I love you."

"You never loved me. If you did, I would have never been here. Do what you have to do, Carmine. I'll wait for you in the hallway."

The truth was, I just couldn't watch. Something told me that I would miss Mr. Vega. And that thought not only scared me, but it made me feel dirty and demented as well.

Chapter 7

The Price of Entering the Dark Side

Carmine and I went through the Vega home and I watched him kill everyone on the main floor, leaving the girls in the basement for last. It was always funny to me how one minute you could be this person who you thought you knew and, in one fast second, that person could be gone. I was no killer. I was just a girl who was stolen from her mother. I was a girl who spent her days dreaming of a better tomorrow. But that little girl didn't even flinch as blood splattered and almost looked like paint against the white walls of the house of broken dreams. That little girl who just wanted to come to America and become a model to help her mother had died years before, and I was just realizing it.

"Okay, we have to get washed up. I'll use the shower in the master bath and you can use the one in the hallway," I said to Carmine.

Carmine nodded his head and didn't speak a word. He was quiet the whole time, which kind of scared me.

I didn't break down until I was behind the bathroom door. Sitting on the floor, I cried for my mother. I'm not sure how long I stayed there, but with each tear that fell, it was as if I was not just emptying my tear ducts; it was as if I was also emptying my heart. All I wanted to do was make the world feel the pain that I was feeling, just like Mrs. Vega. I wanted them to feel the pain that I was in. I wanted to take from them what had been stripped from me, and that was pure happiness.

After getting myself together, I stood in the mirror looking at myself, trying to recognize the girl who looked back at me, but I couldn't. I felt different inside and wanted my outside to match. I rummaged through the bathroom cabinet and found the late Mrs. Vega's hair dye. I read the instructions on the box and it didn't seem like it would be too hard to bleach and dye my hair, but first I looked for the hair clippers.

I chopped off all of my hair with the scissors and, after, I used the clippers. The back wasn't perfect, but I would have Carmine help me with it once I was done.

It took me a few hours to do my hair and shower. Once I came out of the bathroom and called Carmine, he came into the room with his mouth wide open.

"Does it look that bad?" I asked as I turned and looked at myself in the dresser mirror.

He came up behind me and wrapped his hands around my waist. "No, Billie, you look beautiful."

I smiled and asked him to edge up my short new hairdo. After he was done, I added mousse and watched the little curls form on my head.

"Now you really are Billie Blue Blondie," Carmine said.

I smiled as I thought about the woman who seemed to be looking back at me in the mirror. "Just like my mother. I look just like her."

I hugged Carmine again. Nothing else mattered for a little while, not the dead bodies that littered the house, not my dead soul, and not the rest of the lives we were about to take.

Chapter 8

The Price of Being Billie Blue Blondie

Carmine and I stood at the top of the basement steps as we went over what he was going to do down there. When I said that I would never step foot in that cellar unless it was for revenge, I meant it.

"So, what do you want to do with them?" Carmine asked.

I smiled and told him to get me the biggest knife he could find. I didn't really have a plan, but I did know that Erin was going to be all mine. I couldn't care less about the other bullies, but she and I were about to dance to a very deadly rhythm.

Once in the basement, I stood in the middle of the room and surveyed my surroundings. I could smell the fear that was building in the air as Erin spoke up. "What's going on up there? What was all the screaming about?"

I smiled so wide that I was almost sure all of my teeth were showing. "I killed them all. Well, Carmine did most of the dirty work. So now, we only have you three to take care of."

I said this with an air of calmness, as if I was talking about washing my hair. The thing was, the thought of killing them somehow came with ease. There was a driving need to chase the sweet scent of blood that wasn't there before.

"Are you fucking crazy? You can't kill us!"

I didn't answer Sofia. Instead, I made my way to the corner where Erin was chained, and stood in front of her. I poked my chest out with arrogance, and planted my feet to the floor with vengeful pride. I beamed like a queen on her throne as I watched fear engulf Erin's face. Like Carmine, I stood there quietly as I raised the knife and slashed it across Erin's face. Over and over again, I hacked at her scarred skin with pleasure.

Her screams of agony excited me, and before I knew it, she was on her back with her legs wide open. I stood there in amazement watching her reach into her panties. The knife in my hand froze in midair. I was immobilized by my curiosity when I saw Erin rubbing her clit while begging for me to keep cutting her.

"Don't stop now! Come on, Billie, keep going. Cut me, Billie, cut me."

I stood there in bewilderment. I had heard of knife play and BDSM fetish, but I had never seen it play out to this extent. Erin had blood streaming down her face and body yet she wanted more. I watched for a little while longer until Carmine came over and snapped me out of my trance.

"Kill this bitch already. Cutting her turns her on. So stop playing with her."

As Erin drew closer and closer to an orgasm, I became angrier. There I was trying so desperately to inflict pain on one of my tormentors, yet she found enjoyment from it all. So as she wiggled around on the floor, I stuck the knife directly in her throat. I pushed it in as far as I could get it and, before I pulled it out, I looked down between her legs to see if she was still turned on. To my surprise, she was, and I could not wait to pull the knife out of her collarbone and watch her bleed to death.

It didn't take long for her to die once the knife came out of her neck. I stood watching as her fingers played against her clit until her last dying breath. It took me a little time to get my thoughts together. I could not understand how this life we all had come to live could bring us to such a distorted place. I wondered if Erin was ever normal, or if she always had a desire to feel pain, and then turn it into pleasure.

I looked around the room and wanted to ask the other girls about the horrifying secrets they were hiding. I wanted to ask them if this world, our world in captivity, had turned them into monsters too. Truth be told, I knew that all of us were ruined in some way. Erin's devil showed itself in the merging of pain and pleasure. Even as her life was being taken from her, she still felt the need to feed the monster within, and that saddened me. I felt sorry for her, for all of us. We were all victims, and because of that we were now all damaged. While I stood there, I wondered about the demon that hovered above our heads, digging its way to our hearts. Some were born with the devil inside of them. And others, like myself, our angel of darkness would one day appear out of thin air. Soon, we would forsake any sign of humanity, and the devil would become the driving force behind the cruelty we would bestow upon the world.

With me, I knew that I had lost my soul. I knew that after that night nothing would be off-limits. I had no mother, nothing to really live for, nothing to instill the fear of death within me. I also knew that there would be no stopping me. Whatever it was in life, if I wanted it, I was going to do anything to get it, and that also made me worry about Carmine. I knew that even though I loved him, and he loved me, if I had to hurt him to feel alive, I would. And that fact scared me. It was as if standing right there, in that basement, I finally faced the monster that I was hiding within, and I liked her. I fucking loved her, and I was so happy to have met her that night. I knew that freeing her meant that I had just become unstoppable.

"Billie, what are we going to do about the other two?"

I looked at the other two cowardly females who clung to each other for dear life and I decided that they were not even worth my time. "Look at them. Now that I have cut off the head of the beast, they are crumbling. What happened, ladies? Can't hold your own now that Erin is gone?" I asked, but neither of the girls answered.

"Should I break their necks or should we let them burn?" Carmine asked with the look of death in his eyes.

"Let them bitches burn."

As we walked away from Erin's body, Carmine took my hand, but quickly let it go. He walked over to Sofia and grabbed her by her hair. She tried to fight but she was no match for him or the chains that secured her in place. I watched and almost salivated at the sight before me. He twisted and turned her head almost all the way around and didn't even stop when we all heard that pop.

"Carmine, baby, we have to go."

As he let her go, Sofia's body dropped to the ground. It was as if the dark spirit of death had left his body. He walked over to me with clear eyes and a smile. I could tell that standing before me was the sweet Carmine I had grown to love, and I was happy that his devil was now at rest.

"I thought I told you to let them burn," I said with a smile.

Innocence riddled his response. It was as if he was the little boy on that boat again. "I know you did, but . . . she was always so mean to you. I had to do it, Billie. I'm sorry. You're not mad at me, are you?"

I wrapped my arms around his neck while kissing his lips to the sound of Terry screaming for her life. Pulling away from him, I asked the question I already knew the answer to. "No, baby. I'm not mad at all. You will do anything for your Billie, baby, won't you?"

Carmine smiled from ear to ear as he nodded his head up and down.

"And that is why I am in love with you, Carmine. You are very special. And I want you to know that no matter what—"

"Shut the fuck up, bitch!"

Carmine had turned around, and slapped Terry so hard that he knocked her out. Then he turned back to me, and asked me to continue.

"No matter what, Carmine, we will always belong to each other. Promise me that we will die for one another, if it comes to that."

Carmine looked dead into my eyes and said, "You have my word."

There was nothing else to say. I believed him.

As Carmine doused the basement, I took care of the upper floors. I was void of any emotion as I spilled the gasoline over the cook and maid. I even smiled as I gave Mrs. Vega an extra helping of the accelerant. I couldn't wait to turn her body into ash. As I approached her husband, thoughts of our nights in the bed rushed through my mind.

"You really are a sick fuck but, strangely, I will miss you," I said aloud.

When I came up to my buyer, I noticed that his keys had slipped out of his pocket. I picked them up, and kicked him for the hell of it. Then I gave him the same gasoline bath the rest had received. I could hear the lone survivor crying from the floor down below, and my heart began dancing with joy. They all had been cruel to me for no reason whatsoever. I never bothered them and had no reason to. We were all living the same hell.

Making my way to the top of the basement stairs, I called out for Carmine. "Hey, Carmine, are you ready? I want to get out of here."

"Yes. Start the fire on the third floor, and I will light it down here."

A triumphant feeling came over me, and I smiled as Carmine shouted instructions. Then I took a look at Terry and yelled, "I bet you wish you were all a little nicer to me now, huh?"

"Yes!" she screamed as I giggled out loud.

"You can go fuck yourself. It's a little too late for that now. I hope you rotten bitches burn in hell."

I didn't stick around to hear her response. I went to the third floor, lit a match, and tried to burn all of the memories that were formed in that house.

The smoke was getting thick as Carmine and I made our way to the beautiful BMW my buyer left behind. Once inside, I looked around the car taking notes on everything left behind by the buyer, including the gun that was tucked in the glove compartment.

"Do you know how to drive this thing, Carmine?" I asked.

"Yes, one of my dates gave me a few lessons. I'm not a pro, but I'll get us to where we have to be."

Carmine backed out of the driveway, but I wouldn't let him drive away until most of the house was immersed in flames.

"Isn't that just beautiful? It's almost as if I can see their evil souls dancing in the smoke. Just look at it, Carmine. This is the prize of it all. We won the battle of evil," I said.

He looked at me as if he was shocked that my coldness matched his. "I thought that I was the only one who felt this joy. I thought that I was crazy for feeling like this. Watching this fire, it really makes me happy, Billie. I not only killed the people who hurt me, but I killed the people who hurt you, too."

Leaning over, I softly kissed his lips. Then I said, "No, Carmine, you are not alone. I am the happiest that I have been in a long time, and I owe it all to you. I love you, Carmine, and we will be together until the day we die."

I made him park the car across the street from the burning house. As we watched the flames, the sudden need to make love to him emerged. He turned off the engine as I climbed to his side of the car and rode him until we both came.

"No one will ever be able to hurt us again. And if they try, they all will die."

I looked into Carmine's eyes and knew that he meant every word that he spoke. "Let's get out of here. Give me the paper. I'll make the call." I pulled out Mr. Vega's cell phone and dialed the number that belonged to the man in charge.

"What is it? Was there a problem with the buy?" the man in charge asked.

"Yes, there was a big problem, Capello. Mrs. Vega, her husband, the buyer: they are all dead."

There was a brief silence before Capello asked who was at the other end of his phone line.

"I am the new bitch who will be taking over this end of the operation. I am the one who killed them all."

Again, there came a brief silence.

"Look, I am just calling you to see if you would like to take this thing to new heights. I will not be dealing in stolen 'goods.' I want to gather the best of the best and head out West. You can either join me, or watch as I take over." I knew that I was jumping into deep waters. I had no idea who this man was or what he was capable of.

"Who is this?" the man asked again.

"I am the girl who had a price of seven million dollars over her head, the record breaker. Now, if my pussy was worth that much, just imagine what my brain is worth. I am only fifteen years old yet I managed to take out a few of the people who worked for you. Now, you have a choice to make, and I will not ask again." My heart was racing but I refused to show any sign of weakness.

"Do you have a pen?" the man in charge asked.

"Yes, I do, but know this: I am going to meet up with you and I hope that all goes well. We all can live and make a lot of money together; but if you try to kill me, just know that I will not die alone. I will take at least one of you with me."

Capello laughed. "My God, I cannot wait to meet you." His tone was drenched with intrigue.

I took down the address and, before I hung up, I warned him again. "Don't be foolish. Know a good thing when it has fallen in your lap."

"Don't worry. Nothing is going to happen to you. Something tells me that this was meant to be. What is your name so that I can call the gate?"

"Okay, my name is Billie Blondie, and we are on our way," I said as I gave Carmine a nod of assurance.

"Whose phone did you call me from?" he asked. When I told him it was Mr. Vega's cell, he told me to get rid of it once our call was over. He assured me that his people would take care of the car once we arrived to his place. Hanging up the phone, I got out of the car with sirens blaring in the background. I ran over to the burning house, got as close to it as I could, and chucked the cell phone into the flames.

Chapter 9

The Price of Self-reflection

We drove to meet Capello with my mind racing in what seemed like a million different directions. Needless to say, I was conflicted, and I began feeling like I had reached a fork in the road of life and death. Mile after mile, I thought of telling Carmine to turn the car around and drive toward true freedom. We could have driven toward a better life, a life where our bodies belonged to us. To me, that was what being free meant. I wouldn't have to worry about being sold, or having an older man in my bed at night, touching and mind-fucking me. I didn't have a mother to look for but maybe Carmine could have found a way to find his. There were so many ways that we could have changed our future but, instead, we followed the darker path. There was a need in me to meet this Capello man that I didn't even understand at that point.

I should have stopped Carmine but, instead, I let him drive full speed in the direction of the ultimate captor.

Where would this meeting lead me? I was leaping toward becoming what I hated most, and that was a scary feeling. It was scary because, deep down inside, I knew that I wanted to be the one in Mrs. Vega's shoes. I wanted to be in charge. I would make sure to never end up in a situation where I could ever be victimized again. And standing in the free world unchained, I was fearful that there would always be a possibility that I could end up a sex slave, confined to a basement. No matter what it took, I would never let that happen again. To me, I had no choice. This was about assuring our position of power. It didn't matter that I would have to become the monster, as long as I didn't feel the way I did in the Vega home. I tried to tell myself that I would do things differently than she did, but I knew that it wouldn't be easy. I was heading toward the path that enslaved me, but I could not utter the words that would emancipate me from the hellish existence I left behind in that burning house.

I shifted in my seat a few times, not really trying to become comfortable physically, but trying to become more content with my own thoughts on what I had a chance on becoming.

"Are you okay, Billie?" Carmine, being the observant creature he was, noticed the battle I was fighting within.

"I really don't know, honey. I keep asking myself why. Why are we meeting with this guy? He hired the people who enslaved us. Tell me why we're going to meet him." I pretended not knowing, but the truth was I didn't want Carmine to know how truly twisted I was.

I glanced at Carmine for his answer, which would come a few minutes later. I waited and watched him seemingly drift into deep thoughts. His answer made so much sense when it finally came that I didn't feel the need to fill him in on my truth just yet.

"Because, Billie, we are hunters. I do not know what will happen once we meet this man, or why we truly have the desire to come face to face with him. What I do know is that if we don't, it will always haunt us. We will look into his eyes and look for the soul of the devil, just to see if he has one."

I took in a deep breath while looking out of the window. "Carmine, I am truly disgusted with myself."

"You should feel no shame, Billie. You—"

"No, it is not because of what you said. I know that part is true. I do want to face the man who sits at the top of this human trafficking scheme.

What makes me want to rip off my own skin is the thought that is weighing heavily on my mind."

Carmine and I looked into each other's eyes as he slowed the moving vehicle. Something told me that he had an idea of what I was about to say to him. He overheard the conversation I had with Capello.

"I can't for the life of me understand why I am having these thoughts. How could I, once a slave, once considered a commodity, a child stolen from her mother and homeland, how could I even consider asking this man for a position, for a seat at his sleazy table?"

Neither of us spoke as my words sank deep into our psyches. Finally, I had spoken the truth out loud. The situation was fucked up and deserved a few moments of silence.

"So, Carmine, if we are hunters, what or whom is the prey in this situation?"

The car was at a complete stop when he looked at me and answered. "Billie, the messed up part about this is that in many ways, some parts of us, because of what we've been through, will always be the prey. But the beautiful part about it is we are prey who freed ourselves from the clenched jaws of misery, and became soldiers who are ready to die at war. That is why you really want to meet this man. You want to show him that we are warriors. We fought as slaves and if fate leads us toward a seat at his table, we will show them that we are rulers, that we are king and queen."

"What do you call the revolting parts that dwell deep within us? Is there an explanation for the portion of our souls that is willing to take what has been done to us, and do the same to others?" I asked as I turned my head back toward the window, unwilling to face the truth head-on.

Carmine sat and thought about my questions. Then he let the answer slip from his lips with ease. "We call that the ruined fragments of our soul, Billie. The parts that will never heal, not even with all the prayer in the world. We didn't ask for this world, sweetie; we were forced into it. We don't know if the offer to work with him, instead of for him, will even be on the table. This ride and standing in the presence of this man may be our last moments on this earth together. The point is we really don't know what awaits us, Billie. If you don't want to find out, just tell me to turn the car around, and I will do so."

As the last of Carmine's words left his mouth, I had turned to him and looked deep into his eyes. He had all of the right answers, but the rotten parts of me told him to keep on driving toward the unknown. I watched as the putrid parts of him put the car in drive and followed my instructions without hesitation. There we were, two ruined and battered souls, heading toward an even darker destination.

The Middle

Watering the Plants

*Once transformation
Has begun,
If not careful
Destruction may follow*

Chapter 10

The Price of a Deal

We pulled up to our destination and, while waiting for the man at the gate to check the computer for my name, a calm feeling fell upon me. I was nervous, but somehow it was as if I knew that this was meant to happen. I wasn't sure if death awaited Carmine and me, but I was eager to find out.

Once through the gate, I marveled at all of the beautiful homes the Miami gated community offered. I thought the Vegas had a nice place, but their home didn't even compare to what I assumed was Capello's dwelling. It didn't take us long to locate house number 333 on Palm Grove Avenue. We entered the second gate that opened upon our arrival. It was at this point that I felt the butterflies starting to flutter in my belly.

"So, what are the plans?" Carmine asked, parking the car.

I looked around and the first thing I noticed was all of the people standing outside. The grounds of the house were big enough to seclude the neighbors from any noise. All of the trees and walls surrounding the home were high enough to block peering eyes. That frightened me a bit. Capello had enough privacy to easily murder Carmine and me without anyone noticing.

"I don't have a plan, Carmine," I offered. Then pausing to think, I said, "I am going into this with a do-or-die mentality. Are you with me?"

I was praying that my eyes didn't reveal just how unsure I was feeling about this entire thing. When I asked if he was with me, I was not only giving Carmine a way out. I was also giving the whole situation a second thought. Could I do this? Should we even continue? My heart was pumping faster. I knew that one way or the other I had to make a decision.

"Grab the gun and slip it between your legs, at your waistline. They may or may not find it, but at least we'll have something. I'll try to keep a knife on me," he instructed, throwing caution to the wind.

Glancing around, Carmine told me to be as careful as possible when hiding my weapons. It seemed as if all eyes were on us.

I was the first one out of the vehicle. Opening the car door, I cautiously slipped my right leg out and, swiftly after, my left leg. I heard a few men in the crowd of what seemed like ten to fifteen asking, "Who is that?" Once fully out of the car, I stood there looking around, trying to take a head count. I motioned for Carmine to get out of the car. Once he was out, he walked over to me, took my hand, and led me to the front door as whispers and questions bounced off of our backs.

The front door opened before I could even knock. I was staring at a beautiful, tall, dark-skinned woman standing at the entrance with her hands on her hips. I glanced past her and noticed the two humongous men standing behind her.

"Bobby has been waiting for you. David and Bull will frisk you before we get this show on the road."

I was worried the two men would find our concealed weapons. After all, they were working for the man in charge, and surely a man of his caliber would have the best guards working for him. To my surprise, they found nothing.

I wanted to ask the tall woman who she was. Judging from her body language and the way she barked orders at the big men who were patting us down, I knew she belonged there. At that point, there was no urgent need to know her name. I just wanted to know what position she held.

"You're kind of young, aren't you?" the tall lady belted.

"I know," I answered with much attitude.

Rocking back on her heels, she giggled before she said, "You little girls always come in with a chip on your shoulder. Relax. I'm not the enemy. I'm just the boss's girl."

I found it interesting that she made it a point to mention her position. I couldn't have cared less. I wasn't there to fuck her man. I was there to get a job.

"And you old bitches are always intimidated by a beautiful, young girl. Grow up, will you? I'm not here to take your man. I'm here to do business with him. Now, where is your boss at?"

Calling her old was only to get under her skin. She really didn't look a day over twenty-five, but we both knew that she was older than me.

"I should kick your fucking ass. You little bitch!"

I watched as her beautiful face became flushed with anger. Just as she stepped closer to me, I heard a voice call out a name with laughter.

"DeeDee, leave her alone, and let them take a seat first before you start threatening them."

Miss Tall, Dark, and Beautiful took in a deep breath and pointed her finger to the right. Carmine and I didn't move. So DeeDee decided to take the lead, and led us to her man.

The interior of the house was as beautiful as you would expect a home to be in that area code. Marble floors, high ceilings, and expensive furnishings added to the pricey décor. In the oversized armchair sat a tanned, handsome, tall man, with sleek dark hair. His fine features added to his attractive face. His Italian heritage spoke loudly in the manner of style and gesture. He held a glass with dark liquor in his left hand, and his white linen attire coordinated with the Miami night. The moon bounced off the water behind him while the cool breeze danced in the air, adding to the ambiance.

Carmine and I stood in front of him. Neither of us sat until we were requested to do so by Capello's girl.

"So you are the record breaker, huh?"

"Yes," I said.

"And him, who is he?"

"I am the nephew of Mrs. Vega," Carmine said, making the point that he could speak on his own behalf.

Capello smiled and nodded. This clearly showed that he understood the message that Carmine's response sent. "I didn't think that you would really come. That is mighty brave of you, the both of you."

I looked over at Carmine, and noticed the muscles in his jaw tightening. That wasn't a good sign. I took the lead and spoke up, in order to hurry the conversation along and get my point across. "Look, we just came here because we want to replace the people we—"

"Shush!" Capello let out, holding his finger in front of his lips. "Not here, little Billie, not here."

I was confused and offended. Where did he come off calling me little? If we couldn't speak, why was I even invited there?

"Don't worry, we are going to take a little ride," Capello said. Then, turning to one of his men, he asked, "Bull, is the yacht here yet?"

"It will be here in a few minutes. They just sent a message," Bull answered.

"I'm not going on a boat with you," I said, standing up.

"Come on, Billie, trust me. If I wanted to kill you, you would have been dead already. Just come with us. I promise you, it will change your life. Besides, it's a two hundred and fifty—foot yacht, not a cheap-ass boat. You came all of this way to talk to me. You might as well take this chance while you have it."

I looked at Carmine for reassurance. He stood up and walked over to Capello and issued a warning to him. I hoped Capello was paying attention.

"I know that as soon as you laid eyes on us, you underestimated us because of our age. I can only tell you that, in doing so, you've already made a huge mistake. Please don't make another one. Come on, Billie, let us go see what this little man has to say."

Carmine had insulted Capello in the same manner he had insulted me, and I could not help but smile. Standing next to DeeDee, Capello looked like an ant next to a giant, even though he stood at an even five feet nine inches.

The breeze and view from the yacht were spectacular. For a short moment, I forgot my unsightly past, my current situation, and what may be a doomed future, and just enjoyed the spot I sat in. Due to my newly cut hairdo, the wind felt chilly on my scalp. Glancing around at all the opulence surrounding me, I pretended that I was a part of Capello's lifestyle. I couldn't help but think that this was the life my mother envisioned for me.

With the thought of the woman I loved and the reality that I would never lay eyes on her again creeping in the folds of my soul, my mood changed. I went from feeling calm and free to feeling total anger. Shackled to this feeling, I was pushed right back into the darkness that seemed to loom over me.

"So, we are on the yacht. Now what?" I said.

"Why did you really come here, Billie? Did you think that I would just offer you a job, just like that?" Capello asked with a snap of his fingers.

"I asked myself the same question as we drove to your house. To tell you the truth, I mean, it's kind of a fucked-up situation, don't you think? Here I am, a victim of your miserable organization. I should've headed to your house to put a fucking bullet in your head. Mrs. Vega treated me like shit. Kept us locked away in that basement, sold her own goddamn nephew to those cougars, fed us just enough to keep us alive—"

"That is not what my business is about. I had no idea that you were being treated this way!" Capello interrupted.

By that point, I was shaking from head to toe as I thought about what I just escaped. Flushed with uncontrollable rage, I said, "What do you mean this is not what it's about? How the fuck would you know what we, the stolen girls, go through? Don't sit there as if you give a shit. How many times have you stopped and checked in on the girls or guys you sell? You don't give a fuck about what happens to us. We are just a dollar amount to you."

"Now you wait a fucking second, little girl," DeeDee stood with that ever-present hand on her hip before she continued. "Who the fuck are you to come here talking about shit you know nothing about? Bobby isn't even that type of person."

"How would you know what kind of person he is? Are you fucking him because you want to, or are you doing it because you're forced to? Where I come from, we don't have a choice." I could feel the fury boiling inside of me. It was as if every night in that house, every single moment, flashed before me, and I was on the edge.

I could tell that my statement caught DeeDee off guard. Her face softened and she sat back down without another word. "I was just a little girl when they lied to my mother and turned me into a plaything for Mr. Vega. His hands . . . His hands . . ." I looked away from everyone and let my eyes rest on the calm waters the ship floated on. "That man touched me in every place imaginable."

"I thought you were a virgin. Isn't that why your bid was so high?"

I didn't even look at Capello as his question left his mouth. My existence in his world was something that he would never be able to understand. "I was, but that's not the point. That man, that pedophile, he made me think that what he did to me was love, and I believed it. If it weren't for Carmine, I don't even know if I would still be here."

I looked up at the dark sky, and at all of the lights that glittered on the horizon, and I thought about all of the young girls who were out there. My story was just one of so many, but my life story would differ from the others. I silently asked the universe, *Why me?* But I knew that there would never be an answer. I could have asked that a million times, but we would never know why so many of us were dealt a terrible hand while others seemed to flourish from birth.

"Is that why you are here? Are you looking for me to rectify what happened to you, to the both of you? What do you want, money?"

I let my eyes drift from the sky and allowed them to rest in the hollow space known as Capello's eyes. I went on and told him about everything and everyone who was burned in that house. I tried my best to convey to him the damage that had been done. I went into great detail about how and why we killed those bastards, from the Vegas, to the girls in the basement, and right down to the damn cook. After, I tried my best to help him understand why I chose to come to him as it dawned on me in that second.

"I want you to understand that you could never rectify what has been done to us. We are monsters now, and that can never be undone. How could we ever coexist in a world that we know nothing about? We are not normal human beings anymore. The world you took from us, when we were with our mothers, we cannot go back to that. We are here because we have no choice. This is all that we really know, and I will be damned if I stay a slave. As Carmine told me before I walked through your door, we fought as slaves to survive, killing our masters in the process. Once you're freed, the only thing left to do is to become a master yourself. So, yes, I want you to give me the same job the Vegas had, and let me show you that I can do it better."

As I spoke, the big man named Bull came up to Capello and handed him the phone. After a few short questions, he hung up, and turned his attention back to me.

"Your story has panned out. You two really did kill everyone in that house."

"Yes, we did," I answered.

"Well, I guess that only leaves one thing."

While Capello was speaking, I kept my eyes peeled on the big man behind him. I saw his hand reaching into his pants, and so did mine. Moving much quicker than Bull, I slipped my hand down my waistline, pulled out the gun, and aimed for his heart. Instead of killing Bull, I hit him in the left arm. Carmine jumped up, and grabbed DeeDee when the shot rang out. Then he pressed the sharp edge of the knife into her neck. She screamed out in shock. It was then that I realized that all the guns on the main deck were pointed at Carmine and me.

"What in the fuck are you doing, little girl?"

"I'm not your goddamn little girl. What? You didn't think that I was going to let that fat fuck kill us without a fight, did you? I warned you. I told you that I would take out as many of you as possible."

"He wasn't going to shoot you, you fucking idiot."

"Why was he reaching into his pants? I saw him. I was watching."

The situation had reached a fever pitch, and things had gotten out of hand. But I saw Capello smiling even though I was pointing a gun at him, and Carmine was ready to slit his girl-friend's throat.

"You are a live one, aren't you? I like that. I can't tell you why Bull was reaching for his waist, but you're free to ask him."

I looked over at the bleeding man, and then threw my free hand up in the air as if to ask him why.

"It's my personal phone, bitch. I keep it on a waist clip."

I looked Bull over, but because of his weight and oversized clothes, I couldn't see his waistline.

"Drop them."

"What the fuck you mean, motherfucker?"

"Your pants, drop them. Slowly," Carmine directed.

His pants fell to his feet, revealing a cell phone and clip.

"See? No gun. Now apologize to Bull so he can excuse himself and get cleaned up."

My lip curled up, and I rolled my eyes. I uttered a low, "Sorry," while I lowered my gun. Carmine still held on to DeeDee, and I thought that was a good idea.

"What I was about to say was that we could work something out. I don't think you're ready to run your own division, but I have the perfect solution. Now, let DeeDee go before I get upset."

I looked at Carmine, and gave him the nod. Carmine released DeeDee, and she pulled away from him, cursing, all the while rubbing her neck and making her way back to her beloved, Bobby. I took a seat while Carmine walked behind me and remained standing.

"He's very much the protector, isn't he?"

"You damn right. Now get to the point, Capello," Carmine growled.

With a smile, Capello got down to business and said, "I have a lady in L.A. who needs a little help. She is getting old and moves a little slower than she used to. She's becoming forgetful, not keeping track of things the way she should, you know how it goes. I think that it would be a great place for you to start, to really get to know how things work."

I rolled my eyes. Capello wanted me to drive slowly, but I knew I was ready to conquer the fast lanes. "Are you kidding me? You want me to be a nursemaid for some old-ass lady?"

The smile that once sat on Capello's face was now gone. His eyebrow furrowed when he said, "That old lady taught me everything I know. She's one of the best fucking madams I know. You can't expect me to put a child in charge of her own division. You don't know anything about this business—"

"I know enough. I lived it," I said, interrupting him.

"Baby girl, the only thing that you could possibly know about this business is how to make men, or women, have orgasms."

I was insulted, and my flushed face showed it. Remaining as cool as possible, anger seething beneath the smooth veneer of my exterior, I quietly listened.

"No disrespect, Billie, but this is the truth. You were a working girl, and I'm not running some bullshit pimp game. This is the big time. We are not waiting for girls to hop into the back of our cars to hand us their night's taking; we are selling humans. We are providing kings, kingpins, actors, ball players, you name it, with high-end ass. Whatever's their pleasure, we have a girl or guy who will deliver," Capello said.

"Will I be doing what you do? Selling girls in weight?" I asked, looking at him.

There was a big grin plastered all over his face again. He looked me over and said, "Come on, Billie. You have to crawl before you can walk. First you learn, and then you take over a division. After you work hard, and prove yourself, maybe then you will be able to join me."

Although I wanted to start at the top, I knew there was a chance that I would have to climb first. I looked behind me at Carmine, and asked him what he thought. He answered without taking his eyes off the other people in the room. "Whatever you want, Billie. Whatever you want."

"If I shake your hand, there is no going back. I want what is promised to me because I'll work to get it all," I said.

I could feel my heart racing when I realized that Capello had stood up and was walking over to my chair. I stood, looking him dead in the eyes. There were questions swimming around my mind, and I wanted to see what was circulating in his.

"I know that you are something special. I knew it when we spoke. I am a man of my word. I am loyal to those who are loyal to me. I take care of the people who work for me, and I am unwavering. If you shake hands with me and you work for what you want, you will get every last bit of it," Capello said, offering me his hand.

I took it, and said, "You have a deal. Now you can shake Carmine's hand."

Capello walked to Carmine and shook his hand without hesitation. Then I asked, "So, what now?" I took in a breath of relief.

"Now we go shopping."

"I'm not in the mood for new clothes. Just take us back to your house so we can get to L.A." I didn't want to come off rude, but it had been a long day, and the hectic pace was starting to catch up with me.

"We won't be shopping for clothes. We're shopping for fresh meat. We are headed to the buyers' circle in the Bahamas, and I have to drop off some cargo," Capello said to me before continuing. "Bring her out," Capello yelled to his men.

I waited, wondering who would appear. When my eyes landed on her, my heart almost stopped. She was a beautiful little brown girl who looked frightened.

"What . . . what is this?" I asked, almost on the verge of tears.

"She's too young for us. We are going to drop her off and put her on the auction block," Capello answered.

My head started to spin. How could they do this to her? "Can't you just take her back home? She shouldn't be sold. She's not old enough for this," I asked, almost pleading.

"DeeDee, show Billie to the master suite so she can get cleaned up and dressed appropriately. I'm sure you'll find something that will fit her. Carmine, you come with me," Capello barked as if he did not hear me.

I was a little apprehensive leaving Carmine and the little girl. Capello and I had shaken hands, and that meant I should trust him; but with this child entering the picture, something in me just didn't sit right. I stood up and followed DeeDee as I looked back and watched Carmine head in the opposite direction with Capello. The little girl was left with the guards.

Chapter 11

The Price of Assumption

The gun still hung from my fingertips as DeeDee led me to what I assumed was the master suite Capello spoke of. I watched her go into the closet. She kept her eyes on me anytime she was near. She exited the closet with a few dresses hanging from hangers. My lips curled in distaste.

"What? Gucci isn't good enough for you?" she asked with that ever-present hand on her hip.

"It's not that. I'm just tired of always being forced to wear cute little dresses."

DeeDee's face looked as if she understood, and her icy attitude slowly melted. Putting the clothes away, she gave me a knowing look, and said, "Sit down with me, Billie. Let's have a drink."

I didn't answer. I followed her to the lounge area of the room, watched as she poured two drinks, and sat down with her as I waited for her to take a few sips before I touched mine. She looked at my drink, looked at her own, and smiled before emptying her glass.

"That story you told out there was horrendous. Before today, I never really stopped and took the time to really give thought to what Bobby did."

"Yeah, well, let him tell it, he had no idea what we were going through," I said, bringing the glass to my mouth, and swallowing the strong liquor. It burned going down, causing me to make a face. I had never been a fan of strong alcohol. It reminded me of Mr. Vega, and how he would get me drunk before violating me. Just the smell took me to a dark place, but it always made things seem a little easier to deal with.

"Trust me, Billie. If he said he didn't know, he is telling the truth. Bobby is a lot of things, but he wouldn't lie about not knowing."

"But what about this girl? How could he just sell her off? This isn't right."

DeeDee reached across the table, and placed her hand over mine. Her seemingly kind gesture caused me to jump, and I pulled my hand away. It wasn't because I didn't want her to touch me, but her touch was foreign to me. Any affection I received outside of Carmine or my mother belonged to Mr. Vega. His wife never hugged me or showed any compassion. So DeeDee's action scared me a bit. Now realizing that I might have just offended her because of my insecurities, I was instantly embarrassed. My voice was strained and low when I spoke.

"I'm sorry. It's just, I . . . I was totally taken off guard. I didn't mean to pull away like that."

"I understand, Billie. It's okay. Believe me. As far as the kid, Bobby would never take her in as a working girl. He can't just take her back home, either. That would be too risky."

For the first time since meeting her, I looked beyond all of her sass and really looked into her eyes. Something told me that she was telling the truth. "Why? All he has to do is drop her off. If he can't do something that simple, how can you sit there and tell me that he didn't know, or that he would care about what was happening to us?" I asked.

"Because, Billie. I know that man. Plus, he saved me when I was near death, and he didn't have to do that."

I looked at her and asked one short question: "How?"

"It's somewhat of a very long story." She smiled, and then continued. "But I'll try to give you the short version."

DeeDee got up and refilled both our glasses. Then she started telling me about herself. "I started working the streets at a young age.

Things can get a little crazy once you hit that concrete as a child. I started out as an underage stripper, and from there . . ."

DeeDee paused and sipped her drink. She didn't have to finish her sentence. I knew what came next after the strip club. It was prostitution.

"I had linked up with a real asshole for a pimp. He was evil as hell. He would beat us for no damn reason at all. He even killed a girl I had become really close to. Her name was Josie, and it's like, no matter what I try, I just can't forget her."

"Why would you want to forget Josie?" I asked.

"It's not that I want to forget the person. It's just that when I think of her I think of what happened to her. She was so young, so sweet, even for a street girl. She lived a hard life by the time she was sixteen. She was a cute little Puerto Rican girl who came to America with nothing but her looks, a drug addict for a mother, and no education."

"So, what happened?" I asked, watching DeeDee stare into space.

"She died trying to defend me. My pimp was strangling me and she jumped on him to stop him. We put up a good fight for a while, but as we crawled closer and closer to defeating him, he pulled out a knife and stabbed her a few times in her chest. The funny thing is, even as he was on top of her killing her, she still screamed for me to run. She was still trying to protect me."

I sat silently and let her have a moment. I could tell by the tears she fought back and the cracks in her voice, she needed a little time to regain her composure.

"Anyway, as she was losing her life, I ran. I left everything behind and just ran for my life. I ran for the life I thought I had given up on, for the life I thought no longer mattered."

"Is that how you escaped and met Capello?"

"No. That motherfucker caught up with me and continued to beat me with Josie's blood still on his hands. We were behind a liquor store when he caught up to me and beat me to the point I thought he was going to kill me too. When Bobby came from behind the store to see what the yelling was about, I was too weak to even fight back. See, Bobby saved me that night. When he told my pimp to let me go and he wouldn't, Bobby shot his ass and picked me up off the ground."

"I wonder why he even stepped in when he's practically doing the same thing."

DeeDee casually shook her head, brushing off my comment. Then she continued speaking. "I thought I had died and went to heaven. I thought

Bobby was a handsome Italian angel of mercy. Well, I must have passed out in his car because when I woke up, I was in a beautiful bedroom with a woman sitting at the foot of my bed. I spent weeks at that house being nursed back to health. Long story short, after being in his house and realizing what he did for a living, I ended up asking Bobby for a job in his organization, just like you. He told me that he just wanted to help me get better and that I should go back home to my family; but, what in the hell was I going back home to, an abusive father? What was I going to do out in the real world? All I knew was hoeing and sliding my ass up and down on a pole."

"So how did you convince him to let you work for him?" I asked, sipping my drink.

"I told him the same truth I just told you, and he understood. From that day on, I was his. He taught me how to be a woman of class. Had people come in and show me how to dress, how to speak, what fork to use, and how to carry myself. These are the things that you will learn and the things you will have to teach your girls. See, I was just like you. I was in a fucked-up place before Bobby gave me life. This is how I know that he wasn't aware of the conditions you and your boyfriend were living in. I know that man, and to see or know about others suffering is not something that he can tolerate. This is a fucked-up business, but he does try to run it with some level of class and humanity, if that's even possible."

I sat there stunned. We all go through life not really knowing what the person next to us has gone through, or even what hell they may still be living in. When I first met DeeDee, I looked at her as some high-priced piece of pussy the boss kept around for his own pleasure. Now I saw who she was: someone who possibly understood what I was feeling because some parts of her were just like me. Some parts of her soul had been permanently damaged too.

"So, Miss Billie, since you don't want to wear a dress, tell me what you want."

I sat there and thought about her question. Then I said, "I want a suit. You got any?"

"You bet your ass I do," DeeDee answered with a smile. She went back into the closet and came back out with three pantsuits. "White, black, or gray?"

I walked over to her, felt and looked over the suits, and decided on the white one. "What top should I put on under the jacket?" I asked.

DeeDee smiled and went over to the dresser. She pulled out a heavy gold necklace with four thick gold bands hanging, each shorter than the last. "With a body like yours, who needs a top? Just put on these black pasties with this necklace and you'll be ready to go."

My eyes got big when I saw her walking toward me.

"You are strikingly beautiful, and your wardrobe should match. You have a great body, your tits are perky, and you have a nice round ass. Your personality, although young, is very bold, and those eyes, Billie, most would kill for them. Your blond hair sets everything off nicely. So, why not? You want to be a boss one day, right?"

I nodded my head up and down.

"So here is lesson number one. Always try to be the baddest bitch in the room, even if that means shocking them or distracting them with your assets. This shit here, it's a man's game, and it won't be easy for you. Most of the men are pigs and will want to treat you like a working girl. You will have to show them that you are bold and up for the challenge. Show them that by the way you dress, the way you talk, and by the way you'll slit their throats if they try to get out of line, understand?"

With that, I started to undress and asked for a shower. The whole time I got ready, the little girl with the big brown eyes stayed on my mind.

Chapter 12

The Price of the Buyers' Circle

For the second time that night, I found myself standing in front of the mirror, questioning who stared back at me. The only difference then was that I loved the image before me. DeeDee had come into the bathroom once I was done showering and had applied my makeup. She gave me a pair of gold earrings she no longer wore. They almost touched my shoulders, and were the shape of hearts. The ring I wore was shaped like a crown with diamonds, which she said was her gift to me. She said that it should remind me that I was a queen among the peasants I would be forced to work with. At first, I was offended until she told me that she spoke of the men I would one day sit at the table with and not the women who would sell their bodies to make us a profit.

The heels were peep toe, a shimmering gold color, and the bottoms were a red hue. DeeDee said that a real boss bitch always wore five inches or better. At first I thought that I would have trouble walking in the high heels but, after a few steps, walking came with ease.

"We're here, Billie. Are you ready for this?"

I looked at the beautiful woman who reminded me of an amazon, and told her the truth. "I don't think I will ever really be ready, but if everyone waited for the exact moment when they thought they were ready to do something, I have a feeling that most wouldn't do much at all. So yeah, I am about as ready as I will ever be."

Within the short time I spent with DeeDee on the yacht, I started to feel comfortable with her. She didn't force herself on me. It all just happened and flowed beautifully.

When I stepped out of the main cabin, I was nervous and wondered what Carmine would think of me. I hoped he liked the new me as much as I did.

"Where is Carmine?" I asked DeeDee.

My eyes searched the room. Then I saw someone at the bar, and thought that it could be Carmine, but I just couldn't let myself believe it.

"Carmine, Billie is looking for you," DeeDee said, looking in the direction of the bar.

If my eyes weren't stuck in my head, I'm sure that they would have popped out of their sockets. Carmine turned around and before me stood a young man I didn't know physically. His features were still the same, but everything seemed so different. His curly hair melted into his molasses-colored skin with a fresh shape-up to boot. His clothes, although just dark jeans and a white T-shirt, seemed expensive. It looked like the same kind of high-priced T-shirts the young, rich customers would wear and brag about when visiting the Vega house. I admired his white sneakers with the Dolce & Gabbana metal tag on the side. The diamond jewels around his neck and wrist made him look like the king we both knew he was. I wondered how much all of these things cost. I was not familiar with all of the labels and their prices, but had often heard Mrs. Vega mention them as she shopped online.

"Walk over to your man, girl," DeeDee said with a slight nudge.

Our eyes were locked on one another as if we didn't want to miss a second of that moment. Once I reached his side of the ship, he smiled.

"Wow, Billie, you look gorgeous," Carmine said, staring at me lustfully.

I watched as his eyes left mine, and traveled over my body.

"I am speechless, Billie."

"As you should be, Carmine. Billie is fucking beautiful, my God," Capello interrupted.

I smiled from the deepest parts of me and leaned into Carmine before replying in a soft tone. "I am at a loss for words myself."

While Carmine and I made small talk about our new appearances, Capello asked that the girl be brought over to him. When she was near him, I pulled my eyes away from my love, and watched Capello's interaction with the child. First, he inspected her hair, checking for lice I assumed. After, he moved on to her teeth. Satisfied, he asked her to remove her clothes.

"Do you really have to do that?" I asked, feeling as if he was going too far.

"I am not doing this in a perverted way, Billie. I have to make sure that her body isn't full of scars."

As he tugged at her clothes, the little girl started to scream and cry. She fought him as much as she could, until I could no longer take it. I ran to her, pushing DeeDee out of my way. Once I reached her, I pulled her from Capello and pushed her behind me. Carmine came over and took his place behind her, making sure that the girl was also protected from behind.

"I can't let you do this. Can't you see that she is deathly afraid?"

Capello looked at me in frustration. "Billie, you said that you wanted your place in this

world. This is what you may end up having to do.
I take no pleasure in this, believe me."

I didn't give a damn what he said. I was not
going to let this happen. I didn't know what was
waiting for me once I got off the vessel in the
Bahamas. The one thing I did know was that this
child would never find out. I grabbed the kid's
hand and refused to let go.

Capello did everything he could to get me to
calm down and let go of the little girl, but I just
couldn't. I was so wrapped up with making sure
I stayed beside her that I hadn't even realized
that she was holding on to me for dear life too.

"What am I going to do with this little girl,
Billie? She looks like she wasn't taken care of too
well. She's too skinny, and—"

"Let me worry about that, Capello. Please, you
have to give her to me. Earlier on tonight, you
asked me how you could make up for what was
done to me, right?"

"Yes," Capello replied with a face that let me
know he regretted ever uttering those words to
me.

"This is it. This is what you have to do. You will
never be able to erase the things that were done
to me, done to us. But if you give me this child,
I could make sure that what was done to us will
never be done to her. This is the only thing that

you can do that will ever bring you close enough to redemption. Please, I am begging you."

"But, they are expecting her. She is to be put up for sale. If I don't, I will have to pay for her."

By that point, tears were running down my face. I felt connected with that child, and I was not leaving without her. It was as if I was staring at a younger me: the scared, confused, and unsure me. I was once in her shoes, and I knew exactly what she was feeling. I had to save her, because I was unable to save myself. I got on my knees before Capello and lowered my head. I said a silent prayer to God not knowing that those talks with the Man Upstairs would take a dark turn from that point on.

God, I know that I have cursed at you, told you that I hated you for what you let happen to me, but I need you right now. I am not coming to you for myself, as I have noticed that you have chosen not to answer my prayers. I am coming to you on behalf of this little girl. I do not know her, or know why you have dealt her the same miserable hand as me but, God, I need you to help her. You are the only one who knows what will happen to her if she does not leave with me. If it's anything close to what I have experienced, I beg you to show up here today, God. I know you hate me, and I am not

*too fond of you, but I beg you, God, not for me,
but for this innocent little girl, hear my cries
today, God, please, I beg you.*

I waited, and waited, and I continued to beg
a God I wasn't so sure even cared to listen. As I
inched my way closer to giving up, I heard the
voice of an angel.

"I really think that you owe her this one, Bobby.
Just buy the girl. What do you care? It will be
Billie's responsibility."

I looked up and saw DeeDee turn Capello into
mush as she gazed into his eyes. I could see his
inner battle but, soon, his heart would win.

"Fine, she's yours. But this brings us close to
being even, right?"

I rose to my feet and answered him through
tears. "Yes, yes, this brings you closer," I answered, leading the little girl to a chair. I sat
down, pulled her on my lap, and held on to her
until we reached our destination.

"Billie, she can't come in with us. You will have
to leave her on the yacht."

Instantly, I panicked. I didn't know if I could
trust that nothing would happen to her. "But . . .
but, Capello, please. I don't want to leave her.
What if—" I was starting to sweat and worry
showed itself on my face as Capello interrupted
me.

"Billie, you are going to have to trust me if we are going to work together. She will be safe and waiting for you when you get back."

I stood and thought about things. "Can't I stay with her while you go with Carmine?" I was desperate.

"No, Billie. If you want to join the Pricey organization, you must come and witness this for yourself," Capello answered.

I was left with no choice. I turned to the little brown-eyed girl and told her that I would be back. When she wouldn't let go of my hand, I promised her that she was safe, and that I would return.

When we exited the ship, a man asked for our passports and I got nervous, not realizing that in the underground world money held the equivalence of almost everything. I watched as one of Capello's men handed the guard a stack of cash. It silenced him, and the money allowed us to pass without any documentation. Waiting for us were a couple of helicopters. Then we took a short ride, and soon we were landing on top of a house.

"There are a few things that you two need to know. We are already late so I am going to run through this fast. One, what you are about to see should never be discussed outside of our organization. You may see famous faces, congressmen, world leaders, terrorists, you name it, they may be in there. If you recognize a face, act as if you don't. Because you are new, do not ask anyone else questions besides me. You don't want to look like you don't know what you are doing. Just watch me, and I'm sure you will catch on. Lastly, do not talk to the girls, got it?"

Carmine and I both nodded our heads in agreement and, from there, we exited the helicopter. Something in me was excited. I was curious and wanted to see how all of this actually played out. When I was taken from my mother, I wasn't sold at auction. I went straight to the Vegas' home. I held Carmine's hand as we descended the stairs, went through a short tunnel, and arrived at a door where Capello's arm was scanned under a black light revealing a hidden tattoo. I tried to see what was on the machine's monitor but I didn't move fast enough.

Once inside the lavish home, we were led through a hidden wall, to an elevator, and through another small tunnel. The level of security, precautions, and secrecy had my heart racing. I was coming face to face with the fact that this was not a game. I was in the middle of one of the largest underground sex slave operations, and I was vying for a piece of it.

At the last door, Capello's arm was scanned again while the rest of us received stamps on the back of our hands, also invisible to the human eye.

"Are you two ready?" Capello asked.

"Born ready," I answered with all the confidence that I could muster.

I took a quick glimpse in DeeDee's direction and saw her giving me a nod of approval. When the doors before me opened, I took in a deep breath, and strolled inside.

The all-white room was large with very bright lights. I counted fifty young boys and girls standing on podiums. There were slabs of clear plastic beds beside them. All of them were naked, young, and dead behind the eyes. Men and women walked around the room, pointing and speaking about them as if they were caged animals.

"This is the part where you get to walk around, and see if any of them pique your interest. After that you will be able to inspect them closely. But for now, no touching," Capello explained in a whisper.

I held on to Carmine's hand tightly. I felt as if my knees would buckle. Walking to each podium, I was silently weeping for the young souls who were forever lost. This was not what I wanted to do. I wanted the people I worked with to have a choice. I didn't want to do what the Vegas did. I wanted to do things my way, so I voiced my concerns to Capello.

"I don't want to enslave these kids, Capello. I want to work with people who are willing to do this." I knew it sounded naive but I was hoping that there would be a way.

"Billie, I will try my best to make that happen for you but, right now, it's just not possible. We have to leave here with three girls for the house you are going to and what you want just isn't a possibility right now."

"But—"

"There are no buts, Billie. This is what it is. I promise you that later on we will try to get things to the way you want them. This is the learning curve right now, so I am going to need you to be a student. I have already pushed you past a few levels. Most madams who run their division never enter the buyers' circle. They just get what we send them. This is a privilege not many get to experience."

I looked around and realized that no matter what I wanted at that point, the reality was I wasn't going to get it. He had already done one favor for me and, I guessed, to him that was enough. I would not be walking out of that compound with free-willed sex workers. I was going to walk out with slaves.

"You sure you want to do this, Billie?" Carmine asked in my ear.

"It's too late to go back now," I answered, taking a step forward, and moving on to the next platform.

After walking around for about twenty minutes, the man standing in the middle of the room with a microphone made an announcement: "We are now entering phase two. Please make sure to drop off your selection sheet so that we can get the cargo ready to move on to the next phase."

One of Capello's men walked over to a drop box, and slid Capello's sheet into it. Waiters walked around refilling the champagne glasses of buyers waiting for the cargo of humans to take their places on the clear plastic beds.

"Here is where you get to inspect them. You will be provided with gloves, lights, and anything else you may need to really check them out," Capello offered.

"What do you mean, 'inspect'? What are we looking for?" Carmine inquired.

"Just pay attention and you will see. I asked to look at five girls. You will see what I mean."

Carmine and I stayed quiet as we waited for phase two. With a sound of a bell, the cargo got on the plastic beds. I watched them for any sign of emotion, and all but one seemed lifeless, without thought, and without feelings. I watched the young girl who could not be any older than eight.

She was a cute little white girl who had on too much makeup. Her hair had been straightened and hung past her shoulders. It was as if her quivering top lip pulled me into her world, and into her body. All I could do was think about the little girl I left behind on the yacht. I watched as streams of tears ran down each side of her beautiful blue eyes, and formed puddles on the plastic under her. There she was, in a room filled with strangers who gawked at her on the hard bed. She was stripped of not only her clothes, but also her human dignity.

I wondered what the people in the room looked like to her. Had we lost our human appearance and donned the faces of beasts? What was running through her mind as she looked up at the bright lights above her head? Did she try to envision the home she left behind? I knew she was afraid, but what was that fear going to do to her? Would she break, would she persevere or, worse, would she end up like me? Would she become the same monster she stared out at, wondering how we could be so evil, yet later transform into one herself?

"You may begin to inspect the cargo. Please be thorough and gentle. Remember, all sales are final. So please, make sure to ask questions now and look over everything completely."

I looked at the man with the microphone again and decided that I hated his voice. He was a small man, both in height and weight. He wore a slim mustache, and what hair he had left was slicked back. His voice was high pitched and whiny. I wanted to tell him to shut the fuck up, but I knew that I couldn't. I was becoming irritable and hoped that things would move along quickly so we could get out of there.

We followed Capello to the first girl and stood back and watched. "She is a beauty. Let's take a look at her stats," Capello said as he picked up the clipboard that hung from his number one pick's bed.

"She is sixteen years old and of Dutch descent. She has been working for one year, but ran away from her last buyer and was caught by the hounds. She refuses dates and can become violent."

I laughed as Capello went on to read the Dutch's rap sheet. She was feisty, and it made me happy to think that she was giving them hell. Capello decided that she was too much of a risk and moved on to the next girl on his list: a seventeen-year-old African girl who was taken while on her way to school in London. She was fresh off the boat and looked as if she was trying to will herself back home, as she stared into space.

While Capello went over her information, my eyes found their way back to the white child. No one was inspecting her yet so I breathed a sigh of relief.

"First, we check her mouth and ears. You can always fix cavities but when their teeth are really messed up, it takes time away from getting them booked straightaway. Her card says that she has been tested and is clean but I also look for sores, horrible skin, and scars. I try to get these girls as close to perfect as I can get them."

I looked at Carmine and couldn't tell if he was becoming as uncomfortable as me, but still we pushed on.

"Now, we take a look at her insides," Capello said as he instructed the girl to spread her legs and hold up her knees.

"Is that really necessary?" I asked as my head started to pound. Between this and the kid I left behind on the ship, I felt sick.

"Yes, it is. You want to look in there, feel around to make sure that she has good control of her muscles. You want to make sure that she can get wet and turned on. I like for my clients to feel as if what is happening is real, as if the girls are enjoying themselves."

I turned my head as Capello slid the Cusco speculum—a gynecological instrument that sat beside each of the beds along with gloves and flashlights—inside of the young girl. Although I could not see what was going on, her groans told the story of a girl who was extremely uncomfortable.

"Okay, now we test her ability to make things feel real," Capello added as he pulled the metal from the girl's vagina and slipped on a glove.

I watched as he inserted his fingers in the girl and asked her to hug his digits with her insides. After, he tried to turn the girl on by rubbing her clit with his thumb while sliding his finger in and out of her.

"Yessss, there you are. There you are. You're a good girl. Look at that, getting wet on cue."

At this point, my stomach started to dance. I felt as if I was about to throw up right then and there. I searched for air as my mouth went sour.

"Carmine, take her to the bathroom. Over there on the left," Capello said as if I was embarrassing him.

With help from Carmine, I started on my way to the restroom. Everything was starting to become a blur. All of the faces, all of the voices, they were all becoming distant until I heard her cries. I would never be able to explain it but, instantly, I knew who that voice belonged to. I stopped walking and searched the room for her, as I was somewhat discombobulated. When my eyes landed on her, it made me want to kill everyone in that room. A presumed buyer was trying to pull her legs apart as she fought him off. When he realized that he could not get her to cooperate, he called for the help of the bodyguards scattered around the room. When they moved, I moved.

I ran to her aid, ignoring all the instructions given to us by Capello. It was something that I just could not help. In her, I saw me, even though I was never directly in her shoes. I wanted to protect her/me. I wanted to save her from dying within. I didn't want to be a bystander as they killed what was left of her.

"Get your fucking hands off of her!" I yelled as I reached her and pushed the buyer away from her legs. Carmine was right by my side as the guards swooped in and tried to get the situation under control. Capello looked our way and came running once he saw me sitting on the plastic bed trying to shield the young girl.

"Billie, what the fuck are you doing?" Capello asked with DeeDee and his men behind him.

"I just had to help her. I just had to help," I repeated.

"You can't do this, Billie. You have to get up," Capello said as he tugged at my arm.

"I want to buy her. You have to get her for me."

I was frantic. I could feel my eyes scanning the room at a fast pace; and I watched as my body shook violently. I was losing control. The thought of that little girl being thrown into the evil world I had just escaped was bringing me to the brink of insanity. The man with the microphone came over to us in hopes of calming everyone down.

"Sir, sir, please get your guest under control."

"Motherfucker, don't you think I know that? I'm a fucking partner in this business, not a fucking worker. I don't really have to do shit I don't want to. I just do it to keep things fair. I know the damn rules."

"I'm not leaving without her!" I screamed to the man with the annoying voice.

For a second time that night, Capello tried his best to calm me down. Soon, he would grow tired of my shenanigans and give it to me straight.

"Billie, I'm sorry but you can't save them all. I have already given you one. I can't give you anymore tonight. I'm sorry."

I was heartbroken, but the truth was staring at me through the eyes of Capello. Looking at the blond beauty and with tears rushing from my eyes, I told her that I was sorry. She started to scream and cry as she clung to me. Unlike the lucky soul on the yacht, I had to push her from me and walk away.

Once back on the floating vessel, I held on to the only soul I was able to save that night. My mind would drift back to the blue-eyed child I left behind as the waves crashed against the boat, but I told myself to just concentrate on the one in my lap.

I was sure Capello wanted to hide the fact that my fight for the little girl touched his heart, but he couldn't. It was written all over his face.

"You would rather die than to have let me sell her, huh?" Capello asked, speaking of the child in my lap.

I was staring at Capello's face. I looked deep into his eyes, and gave him the most honest answer that I could muster. "Kill or die; either way would have been worth the fight to save her."

A few hours later, we were headed for the airport. There, we boarded a jet destined for Los Angeles, California.

Chapter 13

The Price of Meeting Bellissima Buzzelli

By the time we landed and got into the waiting car, my eyes were burning. I was exhausted, mind, body, and spirit. Capello kept going on about the woman we were about to meet while I faded in and out of la-la land.

"Billie, this is important stuff. This lady is no joke. She demands respect at all times. She's old school when it comes to this. She isn't too happy that I am bringing someone in to, essentially, take her place so I'm sure she's going to be nasty to you."

I turned to Carmine, and he looked equally as tired as me, but I still managed to smile. "Where we come from, mean is an everyday occurrence," I answered.

Capello laughed and continued with his warnings. "Well, don't try to pull any of that funny shit you pulled at the buyers' circle 'cause I'll be picking up your body in trash bags. Do you hear me? This is one crazy old bitch, but one of the baddest I have seen."

Capello went on to warn the three girls he had acquired at the auction about running away, or trying any funny business. He told them that girls at that house never got second chances; and, if they proved themselves to Bellissima, they could end up living on their own while working for the company. I looked at Capello and let my mouth move faster than my brain.

"That's if they don't get sold off to some prince or sick fuck who is looking for a sex slave?" I asked.

Before answering, Capello took in a deep breath. Then he said, "There are different levels in this organization. There are girls who are bought to be sold to, as you say, princes or to remain slaves. There are girls who are sent to brothels and sold to pimps. Then, there is the top-rate flesh market. We take these young boys and girls and teach them how to be classy. We teach them about different countries and their cultures. We make them bilingual and make sure they are adorned with the finest things in life. They are considered top shelf."

"If it's such a great life, why force people to do it? Why not have people who are willing to sell their bodies and souls work for you?"

"We do have that, too. Not all of our workers are . . ."

It seemed as if Capello couldn't bring himself to utter the truth. So I did it for him. I leaned forward and spat out the reality of the operation that, at the auction, he so proudly announced he was a partner in: "Stolen, we are stolen and kidnapped. But hey, I guess having some who are willing balances out the ones who are forced."

The rest of the ride was quiet.

The grounds of what would be our new home was just as extravagant and well secured as Capello's waterfront home in Miami. My nervousness, unlike the night before, was dissipating and now I was severely yearning for some rest. We exited the vehicles, and the three girls Capello bought at the auction were led away.

DeeDee, Carmine, the girl I rescued, and I were escorted through the front door of the home. We walked to the back of the house where a lavish spread of breakfast awaited us on the back terrace. We took our seats and waited. I thought about asking the kid her name but opted to wait for a moment when we were alone.

I heard Bellissima before I saw her. Loud thudding sounds from her walker echoed through the house, announcing her arrival. When she came into sight, there was confusion on her face. Capello stood up, greeted her, and offered the explanation to the forgetful, elderly woman of why we were at the table.

"Bellissima, I want you to meet Billie and Carmine. They are here to get training from you."

She looked us over, starting at our feet and ending on our faces. When I looked into her dark eyes, they seemed empty. Her long silver hair hung down her back while her small frame hovered over the walker. She wasn't a beautiful woman with her oversized snout and a face filled with moles, but her presence demanded respect, even at her age.

"Training for what?" she asked with a curl of her lip, looking as if she had just smelled a foul odor.

"I want you to show them how to run the business. We already had this conversation, Bellissima. I called you from the airport. Don't you remember?" Capello answered as he looked to us with a glance that said, "Stay calm; she's just a little scatterbrained."

"You bring them, this Negro trash, to my table and after you tell me to train them to replace me? Didn't I teach you better than this? I don't care about a phone call. I will not do this," Bellissima answered.

Out of anger, her once unnoticeable Italian accent would spill through her words and deceive her. My level of irritation with Bellissima rose due to her harsh words. Knowing that I was sleep deprived and hungry, I decided it was best to keep my mouth shut. I had a feeling I would have plenty of opportunities later on to put this woman in her place.

"You are getting old, Bellissima. There is no getting around that. You are at the end of your reign here and I need you to do this."

DeeDee leaned into me as if she knew that I would only be able to take so much of the unpleasant, old lady. "Remember what Bobby told you. She's mean as hell, but if you listen to her, you will end up being the best. I can't hardly stand the bitch but she is, well, was great at what she does."

I didn't answer. Instead, I went back to listen to the conversation between the old bat and Capello, which had turned into a screaming match in Italian. It must have gone on for another ten minutes before Capello yelled something I could not understand while he slammed his fist into the table. With that, Bellissima looked our way and asked, "Which'ah one?"

"The girl," Capello answered.

Bellissima slowly made her way to me, yanked at my arm to get me to stand up, and just stared at me once we were face to face. This lasted for a few minutes. Without taking her eyes off of me, she addressed Capello. "I will'ah do it, but this is not the one."

Glaring into her dark eyes, I answered for myself. "Yes, I am. I am the only one."

Again her face scrunched up as if she was disgusted. With a nudge from her, I was instructed to sit back down, and I did. As she left the terrace, Capello tried to get her to stay, but that was a losing battle. She told him that she would be in her room and that he should stop in to see her before he left.

Once the witch flew out of the room on her broom, we ate, spoke very little, and were shown to our rooms. My new little friend stayed quiet the whole time and it was then I realized that she had yet to utter a word.

"These are your rooms. I called ahead and asked them to give you the room with the Jack and Jill bathroom. I was certain that you would want to stay close to the girl," Capello said as he showed us the two bedrooms and bath.

I offered him a simple, "Thanks."

"So what are you going to do with her? You don't want her to work and since she is what we will call my gift to you, you owe me nothing for her."

I looked at the young girl and realized that I didn't have an answer. What was I going to do with her now that I saved her? I had even asked myself that same question earlier while watching her eat as if she was starved.

"I don't know yet, but I'll be sure to let you know," I answered as I ran my hands through her pretty hair. She leaned into me, and at that moment, I knew she felt safe. Kids were funny that way. All you had to do was show them a little kindness, and you had their trust. That was when it hit me that I hadn't spoken to her much. But I was too wrapped up with what was going on around me to really hold a conversation with her. In a crazy way, I was her, and she was me. We were both traveling on a new road with no idea of what our destination would be.

"Okay, you two will be provided with cell phones with my number already programmed in them. Look for the name Alvaldo and that will lead you to me. In the closets you will find clothes for the three of you. If anything doesn't fit, just let one of the house workers know."

"Wait, you're leaving already?" I asked as if I was a kid whose father was leaving to go to work.

"I have other business to attend to. Don't worry, if you listen to Bellissima, you will be fine. Ignore her bullshit but pay attention to what she tells you."

I looked at DeeDee and she smiled. "Take my number, Billie. If you need to talk, I'm here for you."

Capello and DeeDee walked over to Carmine, shook his hand, and told him to try to keep me calm while dealing with the wicked witch. After they said their good-byes to us, they went to the room at the end of the hall to speak with Bellissima.

Chapter 14

The Price of Responsibility

I sat at the edge of the bed trying to understand what I was feeling. I was in a melancholy mood, which left me feeling indifferent. Within less than forty-eight hours, our position in life had changed. We were no longer slaves, and I had even managed to rip someone's life from the claws of hell; yet, I wondered when true happiness would seek me out and grab a hold of me.

I looked at the small hands that I had wrapped in mine and wanted to know more about her. "What's your name?" I asked her.

When she answered, her tone was so low that I had to strain to hear her. Her accent told me that she was from an island. "My name is Zen, Miss Billie."

Hearing my name leave her mouth flooded me with emotion. "How . . . how old are you?"

I asked as my voice cracked and I fought back tears.

"I am eleven years old."

Swallowing down vomit, I asked her where she was from.

"I lived in the Virgin Islands, but they told me that I could never go back. They said my mom and dad were killed in a car accident and that's why they were picking me up. I was on my way home when the woman stopped me. I was so sad, Miss Billie. I'm not supposed to get in the car with strangers, but they told me that no one was going to be home since my parents were dead."

I couldn't speak anymore. I had begun to tremble as my tears were begging me to set them free. How evil could these people be? All I could think about was her parents worrying about her, wondering why their little girl never came home.

I hugged Zen tightly, hoping that my arms offered her some sort of comfort. I did not express my feelings to her verbally. Instead, I chose to show her love with my arms.

"Why don't you let Zen wash up so we can all get some rest?" Carmine asked after a short while.

I walked Zen to her bedroom, pulled out a beautiful pink nightgown, although it was day, and led her to the bathroom. Even though my words were limited, I tried to convey something to her that would put her little heart at ease.

"Everything will be okay now. You're with me, and I won't let anything happen to you, okay?"

For the first time, Zen smiled at me. She got close to me and wrapped her arms around my waist and asked, "Can you and the nice man be my mommy and daddy now, since I don't have them anymore?"

With that one question, my tears were released forcefully. Carmine and I were children ourselves. Giving into our vengeful desires to get even with our evil guardians was easy. Being asked to take on such a great responsibility was not. I embraced both Zen and her question wholeheartedly and honestly.

"I don't know, Zen. We can certainly try."

Walking out of the bathroom, I entered the bedroom, and immediately fell into Carmine's arms. I told him what transpired in the bathroom with Zen with the hope that he would agree to help look after her. He stayed pretty quiet throughout the whole ordeal and I desperately wanted to know what he was thinking.

"Billie, whatever you want to do, I'm with you," Carmine said as I stood in his arms.

I pulled away from him, but made sure his arms were still around my waist. I asked what he was thinking as I looked into his eyes. It took him a little while to answer.

"I'm thinking that, because of you, I am free. If it weren't for your plan at my aunt's house, you would have been sold off and I would still be enslaved for women to use me."

"But, Carmine, I couldn't have done it without you. It is because of *us* that *we* are free. I can't thank you enough."

He smiled and, in that very moment, I learned the importance of breathing life into your mate. I could have stood there and taken all of the credit, but that would have been wrong, untruthful, and would have stripped him of the boost I had added to his pride.

I leaned in and kissed my king for the first time since the last. Finally, a smidge of happiness crept up my spine.

"Miss Billie, I'm ready to go to sleep now," Zen called out from the Jack and Jill bathroom door.

I walked into the restroom and smiled at how cute she looked. I pulled her hair back and put it in one big braid, just like my mother used to for me. The thought made me smile. My mother was always my safe place. Even while living in terror, my memories of her would keep me sane. Remembering her smile, her voice, even her rough hands made the world a little more bearable.

After braiding her hair, I walked her to her bedroom. As we stood by her bed, she looked nervous.

"What's the matter, Zen?"

She looked unhappier as she answered. "I'm scared to sleep here by myself. I don't know this place," she answered, slipping her hand into mine.

"Do you want to sleep with us?" I asked.

She smiled and I knew that I had my answer. I took her back to our room and told Carmine that I was going to lie with her until she fell asleep. After, I would have him transfer her into her own bed, so that I could bathe.

Carmine smiled and headed for the bathroom to shower. I wasn't sure when I had fallen asleep but I didn't open my eyes until the next morning when Carmine woke me up. I guess I really was exhausted by the end of my quest to be free.

Chapter 15

Carmine

The Price of a Lover's Heart

When I came out of the shower, Billie and Zen were fast asleep. I thought about waking her, but I knew that she was drained and in need of rest. Although sleepy myself, my mind would not let me doze off. I needed a drink and a joint. That always seemed to work when I spent time with Mrs. Rachel.

She was one of the women I actually liked spending time with. She was a forty-year-old woman who was still full of youth. When I would go off with her, it gave me a false sense of freedom, which I didn't mind experiencing. Every time she dropped me off back at the Vega house, I often wondered why I didn't just run away while I was out with her. Then it would dawn on me that I would be without Billie. I wouldn't be able to live with that.

I opened the bedroom door and found one of the women who worked in the house. I asked her for a cold beer and whispered about the weed. She smiled and told me that both would be delivered to my room within minutes, and she didn't lie. With a cold beer and two rolled-up joints, I sat in the chair across from the bed and stared at the girl I was deeply in love with. I smoked and drank, and I smiled off and on as I thought of us.

We had done it. We were free, and Billie even managed to get us jobs. She was something else, and being with her gave me confidence in knowing that things would be okay.

Watching her breathe, I thought about who she was, and who she had become because of this whole ordeal. It was scary at times to watch and listen to her, but also it was comforting. Like watching her go one last round with my uncle the night we killed him. It was disturbing, but I guess it was something she felt she had to do. I didn't understand it, but who was I to question her reasons behind it? It wasn't like I hadn't risen from the murkiest corners of despair myself. That was what connected us. Although it wasn't the healthiest form of connection, I didn't feel alone in that dark space that would often terrify me. It was selfish, I know, but it felt good

to have a dark angel by your side when, inside, you felt like the devil.

I had dreamed about killing the people who caused Billie and me so much pain; and, without her, it would have still been a fantasy. But for Billie, I would've hung myself before I watched her feel any kind of pain. I just couldn't help it. I was weak when it came to her.

Even while sitting there in that chair, staring at her made me appreciate her more. Looking far beyond her outer beauty and piercing deep within her soul, I knew that she might just one day be the death of me. *I was and I am still willing to die for her.* My love for Billie ran that deep, and it was like that from the very beginning. I guess it was just written in the stars.

The minute I laid eyes on her, I knew that loving her would not be easy. I also knew that I would probably have no choice. There was something that drew me to her. It was that thing that caused my heart to drop to my feet then jump back up into place. She was frightened, but something about her told me that she possessed the type of soul that could never be broken or defeated. Her beauty stopped me dead in my tracks, but what was radiating from within her kept my interest growing.

During my time at my aunt's house, I had seen a lot of girls come and go. None captivated me like Billie. Even within my own captivity and problems, my mind still wandered back to her, especially on the nights she slept in the rooms upstairs in the Vega home. I knew what was going on between her and my uncle, and I wanted to kill him for it.

I hated the both of them, my aunt and uncle. At night, when Billie was gone and the evening was silent and dark, I would think about my mother and sisters. I missed them deeply, although she gave me up. Even at that young age, I understood why the sight of me angered her, although it hurt like hell. I was born a protector and hero in my own right. I would rather endure all of this pain if it meant that my mother would be happy. Even though there were small parts of me that wanted to hate her, I could not. She did not send me to America with her sister to service women and be turned into a slave. She was lied to, and I prayed that one day I would get to see her again.

Now that we had escaped that horrible house, I especially wanted to see her. I wanted to tell her that I was her son, and that I was there to take care of her like a son should. She wouldn't have to be ashamed of me anymore. Not ashamed of

me or my black skin, because I was going to give her everything she has ever wanted. I wanted to let her know that she wouldn't have to count on anyone but me. Not even Mr. Pallazolo. I wanted to rise and be the hero for the woman I loved but yearned to hate.

Before we left my aunt's house, I took her little black book. I prayed that my mother's number was in there, but something inside of me wasn't ready to look. I couldn't speak to her just yet. I had to wait until I could go before her as a man who had done something with himself. She had big dreams for me when she sent me off to the States, and I wanted to show her that they all came true.

That was why when Billie asked me to help her with her plan, I knew that I didn't have a choice. To me, it had to be fate. We did not go into that night with murder on our minds, but the stench of blood littered the air once I heard Billie's cries. I had not felt that feeling since the night I killed that baby. It had haunted me; over and over again I would see that mother's face. Over and over again, I would hear her words, putting that dark spell on me. So when I stepped into that room, it was as if I had accepted her words and decided that whatever I had become that fateful night on that boat was what I was meant to be.

Imagine accepting fate on the level where denial no longer exists. It's a frightening feeling, but also a feeling of power. To ignore what the world has taught you, as far as right and wrong, and to just be. It is as if you are lawless, without a care, and without boundaries. I almost felt inhuman while killing every living soul in the Vega house. Surprisingly, it was a good thing. I moved like an alien, without sound, without feeling. To me, they were all doomed from the day they decided to tarnish the childhood they stripped from us. As I sliced into their flesh, I wondered if I was born this way but never knew it. I wanted to know if this was the person I was always meant to be, or if it was the doing of the woman on that boat.

I would never have an answer, and that was scary in itself. As I tried to imagine what my future with Billie held, I also questioned the role I would play in not only her life, but this business. We were on the road of the unknown, and that was unsettling. The things I saw the night before should have put the fear of God in me. Instead, I stood before everything that happened, feeling nothing. I was numb to the thought of death by the hands of the man we were going to meet. Capello could have killed us and, for me, I would have gone gracefully. The only life I would have fought for would have been Billie's.

What helped me come to the conclusion that I was dead inside was the buyers' circle. I should have been outraged by what I saw but, because of what I had lived, to me this was just a part of life. That couldn't have been normal. Even as Billie begged to save Zen, the only emotion I felt was toward her, and not the little girl. I wanted her to get what she wanted, even if that was to save Zen. This thought bothered me and I promised myself that I would try to form a bond with the little girl. If Billie cared for her, then so would I. I would do anything to make Billie happy. She deserved to have that; she deserved to truly live. As for me, I feared that I was already dead.

Day turned into night, and I found myself on the same chair. After drinking five beers and smoking a countless number of joints, I was now ready to join Billie and Zen in dreamland. Walking over to the bed, I picked up Zen, and took her to her room. Then I returned, and rested my head alongside Billie's. I watched her chest heave up and down as she quietly breathed, and I couldn't help but wonder if she was dreaming of me. I took a few seconds to ask God to truly allow her to love me. Without her love, I would be hopeless.

I leaned in and stole a few soft kisses from her lips. Her eyes opened as I started to pull away.

No words were spoken, just a look. A look that I thought could shatter the world because with that one look, she devoured me. Billie was my sleeping beauty. She stole my heart and I gave her my mind. Pulling me closer, I felt her soft lips pressing into mine. With my eyes closed, I breathed in deeply and let her kiss consume me. Her lips, her presence, Billie the person was bliss. Knowing her allowed me to become excited. She was dangerous in every way. She was delicate, fragile, and soft in so many other ways.

We kissed and slowly the excitement built. Becoming more aggressive in her touch, I lost all control. My breathing became heavy; the inferno within ignited. With just a simple touch of her flesh, I knew I had to have her. Billie's touch felt weak due to her exhausted state, but her passion was as strong as a lion and pulled me in. Suddenly, I was in a frantic state. I pulled at her clothes, ripping them right off of her skin. I dove in to taste her lips again, only to pull away and finish the job of getting her naked. Animalistic sounds escaped my lips. I left her mouth and leaped down to taste her breast.

"Oh, Carmine. Yes, baby! Yes!"

Her groaning excited me even more as her words swam from her lips and landed between my legs.

Finding my way between her thighs, I implemented what the older ladies taught me well. While sucking and pulling on her clit, I fought to keep her legs from choking me. The more she cried out, the more I pushed my face deeper into her. I wanted to taste every inch of her sweetness while yearning to slide inside of her. It wouldn't take long for me to bring Billie to the brink of ecstasy, but her nectar wouldn't be wasted on my tongue. I wanted to feel the warmth of the infamous Miss Blondie against my rod, and I wanted to explode right along with her.

I was rough when pulling away and turning her on her stomach, which seemed to turn her on even more. This wasn't done purposely. I was just caught up in the rage of love. Yanking her toward me, I rubbed my penis against her wet slit. I yelled out in ecstasy, as the thought of our first time together danced across my memories. I hadn't even entered her, yet I sang like a singer. Ready to sin, I slid in and felt her. It wasn't just her body, but her soul that seemed to glitter.

At first, I held on to her hips, watching as my big, thick black pole invaded her cave, but I wanted to be close to her, so I slid on to her back. Our voices merged in a euphoric melody, and sounded like a choir. We sang to the gods of love, although we fucked as if we were the gods of war.

"I love you, Billie. Do you hear me, baby?" I needed her to know this and I tried to make her feel it with every thrust. "I will kill for you, Billie. I will fucking kill anyone who hurts you," I sang into her ear.

"Yesssss, baby, kill for me, baby. Fuckkkkk, I love you, Carmineeee."

Murder and lust merged, forming a union of sin. As we dug into each other's bodies, we purged our putrid souls for the other to see. As her insides became more wet with each word that slipped from my lips, I told her I loved her and I waited to hear it again.

"Fuckkkk, Carmine, I love you too, babyyyy. Yes, you feel so gooddddd. My angel, my hero, I love you too, baby. I love you tooooo."

Her words sent me into a sex-filled state of fury as I held her close. I felt Billie's body tighten around my rod and I knew that we weren't too far from glory. Together, we let the thought of sanity go, and had orgasms within the land of madness.

Falling asleep in her arms was the perfect ending to the life we left behind, and a flawless beginning of what was meant to be.

Chapter 16

The Price of Learning Lessons

Six months had passed and I felt as if I was losing my mind. My days consisted of what Bellissima called classes. I was in the same class as the working girls. I was learning and had become semi-fluent in French and Spanish, while Carmine dominated the Spanish and struggled with the French. We learned how to eat at the table, trained with etiquette the Queen of England would be proud of. While the girls learned the art of seduction, I was told that I wasn't needed in that class; but I always stayed. I kept DeeDee's words in the back of my mind. Because of her, I knew that dealing with men when it came to business wasn't going to be easy, so seduction would probably come in handy.

I hadn't seen Capello the whole time I was there, and that was becoming a problem. I was getting tired of the tedious bullshit he was forcing me to learn, and dealing with Bellissima was not easy. She was a mean old hag who took pleasure in making everyone's life difficult. Whenever I would slouch, she was right there to slap me on the back and shout something that I couldn't understand. Although she seemed to hate me, she took a small liking to Carmine. At least, that's how it seemed. She wasn't as hard on him as she was on me. It was almost as if, to her, I didn't even have a name. She would just look at me and say, "Not Ready, come here." Not Ready had become my name when it came to Bellissima. That's all she ever called me.

It was a Friday morning and I was not in the mood for Bellissima's bullshit that day. She woke up in a foul mood, which didn't differ from any other day. She hurled insults and swung her walker at anyone who got in her path. That particular morning when she called me by her special name for me, I answered with much attitude.

"What do you want?" I asked as I threw my hand on my hip as DeeDee would.

"You'ah speak'ah to me like this'ah? I know why. We treat you different. Bobby make you a princess. You'ah come here, no work. You take the little girl'ah and make her no work'ah."

"Yeah, that's right. She, Carmine, and I will never work selling pussy or dick. I am here to take your job, remember?"

The look she gave me told me everything I needed to know about what she thought of me. Not working was always a big problem for her. She flew off the hinges when she found out Zen would not be put to work. She said that we were losing good money by making her a little princess, and that Bobby was making a mistake. My answer to her was that decision was not one she could undo.

"Zen will continue with the home school, her dance classes, and whatever the hell else she wants to do, but fucking for cash will never be on the list. She will go to college and become a lawyer. Who knows? Maybe one day I may need her."

She laughed at me from deep down in her gut and offered her favorite insult. "You are not'ah ready, Miss Billie. You will'ah never do it big like'ah me. I make'ah Bobby, and I make him big'ah. You are not'ah the one for this'ah. Never ready."

I was trying to stay respectful to the old lady but she made it so hard. I walked up to her and did the only thing I could without putting my hands on her. I stuck my hand in her face and flipped up my middle finger. As she smiled and called me a big baby, I walked up to my room and texted Capello. After five minutes without a response, I dialed DeeDee's number.

"Hey, girl, how are things going over there?" she asked in a cheerful tone.

"I'm about to go out of my fucking mind. This bitch is driving me crazy. If I wanted to be treated so badly, I would have stayed with the Vegas. I haven't even been out of the house yet. I haven't been able to leave the grounds," I whined into the phone.

"Have you spoken to Bobby?" she asked.

"A few times but I haven't seen him. I need to get out of here at least four times a week. How long will all of this go on? I'm supposed to be free, but I still feel like I'm in a cage."

"Okay, calm down, girl. That old bitch must be giving you hell," she answered, giggling at my situation.

I went on to tell her what had been going on in the house. By the end of my rant, she realized that this was no laughing matter. She asked me to give her five minutes so that she could call Capello and call me back after.

As I waited, Carmine joined me in the room. He offered his silent comfort as his hand interlocked with mine.

"I hope that I didn't make a big mistake by coming here with you guys."

"It was the right thing to do, Billie. Just think, if we didn't, we would have never met Zen," Carmine chimed.

He was right. This hell was worth it just for her. She had become everything to Carmine and me. In the afternoons, after all of her classes, she and Carmine would play on the lavish lawn. I had always hated the heat, so I would sit on the patio and watch. He seemed to cherish her as much as I did, and that touched my heart. It was as if she had brought back the parts of me I thought I had lost. She was so bright, and had adjusted well. As much as I loved her, I wasn't sure if letting her go back home to her parents was on the table. I would have let her. She gave me a reason to open my heart again and that was priceless.

"Hello?" I answered the second the phone rang.

"Hey, girl, I have good news. Bobby is sending a car for you around three. I am going to meet you for lunch and we can go shopping."

"Can Carmine and Zen come?" I asked as a smile spread across my face.

"Sure, you can bring them. I'll see you soon."

After I hung up, I jumped into Carmine's lap and told him the good news.

***

To be out of that house was exhilarating. We ate at a fancy restaurant and shopped without a limit. Zen and Carmine were all smiles as we ate ice cream before heading to the park. Even at such a young age, I felt as if Zen completed our small family of three. While DeeDee and I took a seat on the bench, Carmine headed to the swings with Zen.

"How's she holding up?" DeeDee asked of Zen.

"She's doing better than I could have imagined, honestly. Maybe it's her age but she's doing well. Her grades are great and the home school teacher said that her reading and math levels are far beyond her peers in this country. Plus, she and Carmine are growing closer every day."

"God was looking out for her this time. I'm happy she has you and Carmine. She's one of the lucky ones."

I looked at DeeDee and wished that I could wholeheartedly agree with her.

"What's that look all about?" DeeDee asked.

"I don't know, DeeDee. How could God let this happen to her in the first place? How could He let these horrible things happen to any of us? She told me about her journey to America and it broke me down. They kidnapped her when she was coming from school, threw her in a crate with three other little girls, and put them on a cargo plane. They left them in there for a few days. They got no food, no water, and no bathroom. She told me that by the time they made it to the States, she was covered in urine and tears. Her lips were cracked and bleeding, due to being dehydrated. She was also weak, and could hardly walk. So, tell me, how lucky is she really?"

DeeDee seemed uncomfortable with the conversation but continued with her line of questioning. "What about you and her? Are things running smoothly?"

I thought about it before I answered DeeDee. "The first day we arrived in L.A., she asked if we would be her mommy and daddy. To tell you the truth, it scared the hell out of me. What did I know about raising a kid when I am still a child myself? Well, it turns out I will probably be good at it. I love her, DeeDee. I love her like I have never loved before. I mean, I love Carmine, but with Zen it's different."

I looked at DeeDee and she had tears in her eyes. I nudged her and told her to man up even though I felt emotional about Zen myself.

"It makes me happy to hear that, Billie. I think about you three all the time and I always pray that you all find happiness. The shit you all have been through is enough for one lifetime. I just want great things for you."

I smiled at what was forming into my very first real friendship. Capello walked up and sat beside his girlfriend. He offered a hello while I dug into him about missing my calls.

"You don't understand what it's like in that house. That lady is mean as hell," I said in a childish tone.

Capello laughed as he slapped me on the knee. "Trust me, I totally understand. I was with Bellissima for five long years before I got to branch out. She's mean but, as I said before, she molded me into the man I am today."

My eyes got big when I heard the words "five years" come out of his mouth. "Five freaking years? Oh, hell no! There is no way that I am spending five years with that witch."

I meant what I said and Capello looked as if he knew that. "Don't worry, Billie, I come bearing great news."

Before Capello continued, I called Carmine over and told him to leave Zen on the swings. We waited for him to take a seat beside me before Capello delivered his news.

"After meeting you and Carmine, I did some real thinking. This business has been good to me. It has also been good to my son and wife. It provided them with a lifestyle I wasn't privileged to until I became an adult. Sure, as a child we were well off but we didn't start seeing millions until I became a partner and started to do things differently. It took some getting used to but my father and uncle came around once the money started to pile in. I hate to admit it but, I think my changes made this company go from bad to worse, although unintentional. Not financially, but for our workers. I wanted to grow the family business and turn it into an empire. In doing so, that left room for people like the Vegas to come in and mistreat our workers. While speaking to my father, I found out that when it was just a small operation, he knew most of the workers by name and was able to keep track of how they were being treated. My greed did not allow me to have the same experience."

Capello stopped speaking to light his cigar. I took that time to look at DeeDee with confusion written on my face. She waved my silent question away and that gave me the answer I was looking for. She wasn't his wife, nor was she the mother of his child. I turned away from her and waited for Capello to continue.

"This is all that I have ever known. My father and uncle are in this business, although they only collect the money now, and let everyone else handle the business aspect of it. My grand-father was a player in this world as well. Even with all of that family history tied to this, I think this is the end of the road for me. I have never been arrested, and I have done a lot of shit to get arrested for. And honestly, I have never given thought to the day I would exit. That is, until the day I met you."

I stared into his face and asked him, "Why?" Why out of all of the days he had spent selling stolen children and damaged young women and men, how come the day he met me mattered the most? A few seconds of silence fell upon us as he focused on his answer.

"I have no direct answer for this. As I gave it thought, I considered the reason being the way you begged for Zen's life. Or maybe the disre-gard you two had for your own. Meeting me could have meant death but, your past didn't allow you to care. The past that I had a hand in destroying, came to me that night and stared me right in the face, in the form of you two. You know, after I dropped you off at Bellissima's house the first day you came to L.A., I went to see my father and uncle a few days later. I told them about you two and the story of how we came to meet. The one and most import-ant question they asked me was, 'How could you just throw them into the ring?' They asked me how I knew that you and Carmine would be ready to work in our world. They couldn't understand why I had so much faith in two young kids I had just met. They thought I was crazy. To them, taking you two on to replace Bellissima was a big risk." Capello stopped, took a few puffs of his cigar, and then continued.

"When they asked me why, I didn't want to face the truth and answer them; but I had to. I told them that when I looked in the both of your eyes, especially yours, Billie, they seemed empty. It takes a special kind of person to sit at the top of human trafficking, and the sad part is I knew that you had it in you. Was it because of what you have been through? I will never know, but the lack of a soul, the lack of a conscience lives within you. I also thought of how bothered you were at the buyers' circle, and I realized that what was revolting to you had become an almost everyday occurrence for me. So I was exactly what I saw in your eyes and knew that, soon, you wouldn't be so disturbed by the harsh realities of human trafficking. Although on the surface you were disgusted with what you were seeing, just like me you pushed on and continued on this putrid path."

We all sat silently as his words evoked different emotions within us all.

"I went home after dropping you two off and spent a few days in total isolation after meeting with my family. I needed time to think and get back to being human. As hard as it was to face the truth, the fact was that I was an animal. I had gotten to the point where I felt nothing and I just looked at everything I was doing as . . . I was just doing my job."

"So what took you so long? It's been six long months," I spat out without thinking.

Capello glared at me; but then his face softened. "You don't know the ins and outs of this business, Billie. I had to get things in order for my departure. Most are in place now, so that brings me to you two."

I didn't know why, but my heart skipped a beat when he mentioned Carmine and me. We both waited without a word.

"I want to ask the both of you something. Knowing what you have been through, is this life what you really want? You have lived it, yet I haven't, and I am repulsed by what I have caused. I have tried to figure it out, but for the life of me I just do not know why you would want to do this."

His question rocked me to the core. I had no answer as to why, but my answer would remain the same. "I can only speak for myself and my answer is still yes. If I had the chance, I would not run things the way you did. I have already told you that. As scary as it is, this is what I am now, and this is who this life has made me. I have nothing else to live for. The life I had with my mother is long gone. That dirty bitch Mrs. Vega had her killed as her last-ditch effort to hurt me before she sold me. So, I ask you, why not? I have nothing else."

The look on Capello's face read of disbelief. He was staring at the monster he had inadvertently created, and I was sure it hurt like hell. That was the funny thing about life and the lessons it taught us. Every action would always be followed by a reaction. Every decision we made, from small to big, would ripple into the universe. The hardest thing about that rule of life was not knowing who that wave would hit, what destruction it would cause, and how you would feel once it made its way back to you.

"What about you, Carmine? Is this what you want?"

I didn't look in Carmine's direction as Capello waited for his answer. I did not want him to feel as if he had to cooperate with me just because he loved me. I had always questioned his reasons for following me to this destiny but, that day, I would have an answer.

"Capello, the truth is I am just like you. I am the person you are trying to run away from. Like you, I felt nothing at the buyers' circle, just like I felt nothing when I killed those people at my aunt's house. And just like you, this is just a job to me. I lost my humanity on the boat ride to this country and no amount of self-reflection will ever bring it back. I am here to do a job, not as a slave, but as a boss. So, to answer your question, yes, we are ready to do this."

Again, a short moment of silence fell upon us. The truth had slithered from our mouths and hung in the air like the thick L.A. smog that clogged our lungs.

"I will send a car for you two tonight around eight. The kid can't come, but she'll be okay at the house until you two get back," Capello instructed as he stood to his feet.

"How long will we be gone?" I asked as DeeDee joined her man and rose from the bench.

"Two days," Capello shot back as he and DeeDee made their way to their car. "Your things are in the car. Go home and pack a light bag. See you tonight," Capello shouted over his shoulder.

Carmine called Zen over. She ran to us and wrapped her arms around my waist. "I had so much fun today. Can we do it again?"

I told her yes as I looked into her beautiful brown eyes. I worried about being away from her, fearing that I would miss her too much. Carmine read the worry in my eyes and tried his best to comfort me.

"We will only be gone for a couple days. Don't worry, Billie, she'll be okay."

"I'm sure she will," I answered as I thought of the gun I would leave behind for her. Among the different lessons I made sure Zen learned, target practice was one of them.

Chapter 17

The Price of a Seat at the Table

Telling Zen that we were leaving for a few days was torture. She looked just as sad as I felt.

"Don't worry, Zen, nothing will happen to you while we are gone. You are safe here. Plus, I'll bring you something back. Just tell me, what do you want?"

Finally she had a smile, and that caused me to have the same reaction. "I want a big white teddy bear. I used to have one at home that my daddy bought me. I think it will help me remember him and my mother."

My heart broke the minute those words left her mouth. I thought that she would have asked for a game system or gadget. Instead, she just wanted a taste of home.

Looking around the room, I thought for a second and knew that I still had something left to do. I walked over to the dresser and slid open the bottom drawer. I pulled out the same gun I held up on Capello's yacht and brought it over

to Zen. Carmine took the gun from me and, as I
spoke, he showed her how to use it.

"This is for your protection. If anyone tries to
do anything to you—"

"But I thought you said that I was safe here,"
she said with terror in her eyes.

"You are, Zen. This is just in case. As you know,
there are a lot of mean people in this world so,
just in case, Carmine will show you how to use
it."

"I already know how to use it, remember? I got
this," Zen joked in her cute little accent.

As we all shared laughs, that mean old bitch
came walking into our room. "Your car is here.
Don't keep Bobby waiting."

I could not stand that lady and the sight of her
made my mouth go sour. "Okay, Zen, walk us
downstairs," I instructed.

As we tried to squeeze by Bellissima, she
grabbed Zen's arm. "She doesn't have'ah to go.
She is fine," she spat out.

I grabbed Zen and yanked her away from the
witch. "I don't give a shit what you say. I told her
to come with us to say good-bye and that's just
what she's going to do."

"I am going to have it out with that lady one
day. I can just feel it," I said as we descended
the stairs. While we headed outside, I took the
phone Capello gave us and handed it to Zen.

"Okay, baby girl, keep this with you at all times. If you need me, just click on Alvaldo or DeeDee, and they will give us the phone."

Zen gave me a weak smile as I pulled her in and felt her little arms wrap around my waist.

"Don't be sad, Zen. Your birthday is in four days and I promise you we are going to have so much fun."

She giggled as she walked to Carmine and gave him a big hug. "I can't wait, Billie. Come back soon," she said as we entered the car.

"Go on in, Zen. We will see you soon."

She walked backward as she waved. Her cute little brown face etched itself in my mind and heart. Carmine rolled down the window as we started to drive off.

"Go in the house, Zen. We'll see you soon!" I yelled.

"Okay, Billie. I love you. I love you, Carmine!" she yelled as the last of her little yellow dress disappeared behind the front door.

I looked at Carmine with big, wet eyes. "Did you hear that, Carmine? She loves us."

Carmine smiled and took my hand. "We love her too," he answered.

"But we didn't even get to say it back. Maybe the driver should take us back."

"We have no time for that," the driver answered.

"It's okay, Billie. Just tell her when she calls."

The plane ride to Miami was long, but I got some rest. Everyone seemed to be trapped in their own thoughts as we drove to the Capello compound after leaving the airport. I thought about Zen and wondered why Carmine and I were flown back to Miami; and I was curious as to what was on everyone else's mind.

As we arrived and settled at the house, the maid fixed us drinks while we lounged on the large white couch.

"How are you feeling about this?" DeeDee asked. The men had gone outside to smoke, which gave DeeDee and me time to chitchat.

"I was wondering what we were doing here," I answered honestly.

"Well, since Bobby is going into another business, you have to meet the main players."

"What business is that?" I asked.

"Porn," was all that she offered.

I took a sip of my drink and thought about things before I responded. "Why would he want to do that? Porn, prostitution, isn't it all the same?"

DeeDee smiled while shaking her head no. "To keep shit real with you, I kind of talked him into it. I started out as a sex worker and by

chance I met him. My dream as a kid was to be
famous, but I have since let go of that dream.
When Bobby said that he wanted to walk away
from this illegal stuff, I put the bug in his ear."

"But why?" I asked, still confused.

"Because, this will be my shot to make it big. I
want to be a star, and if fucking on film is going
to get me that shine, I'll take it."

I almost choked on the drink I had just taken
into my mouth. "So, you are going to be in the
movies? Is Capello okay with that?"

"It won't be my first time. I did a few flicks
while working for my pimp. Plus, he gets turned
on when he watches me fuck other men."

My eyes felt as if they would pop out of my
head.

"Don't look so shocked, Billie. Some men get
turned on by a beautiful body in front of them,
while others like to know their mate can and will
fuck someone else. Plus, Bobby's family has had
a company called Fantasy Pictures for a while.
He has always run things from a distance. It will
be full time now."

I didn't know what to say, so I said nothing.
How could I judge her? My choice was to continue playing in human trafficking while she
opted to fuck on film. We all had our demons;
they just wore different clothes.

"Don't think too hard about it, Billie. There are things that another person will never under-stand outside of you. Just enjoy today because, tomorrow, you are going to face the sharks."

We all did just that. By the time I called Zen, she didn't answer. It was one in the morning in Miami, and I had to be reminded by Carmine that our time zone was different. Realizing it was past Zen's nine o'clock bedtime in L.A., we headed to bed a bit drunk but rested for the day ahead of us.

The next day, I went shopping with DeeDee. The prices in the shops she took me to blew my mind, but she told me that Capello was footing the bill and to get whatever I wanted. I bought clothes for my small family and made sure to pick up things for Zen's birthday, including her teddy bear.

While at the jewelry store, three pieces of jew-elry caught my attention and made me wonder if they were meant to be sold as a set. One was a necklace with a heart-shaped pendent and a smaller heart-shaped hole in the middle. Beside it was the little missing heart with a keyhole in the middle, and on the right of that was the key. I called the jeweler over and asked him if it was a set.

"They can be, or you can just buy one piece," he answered.

I smiled at DeeDee and told her that I wasn't leaving without the set. I told her that I would work it off if she got them for me, which made me silently question when I was going to start making money on my own. She told me that I didn't have to pay Capello back, but with the hefty price tag of $40,000 for the set, I was sure that I would end up working it off in an indirect way.

I didn't let Carmine know about the gifts. I figured that I would give both him and Zen their presents at the same time. As we showered and dressed to meet the partners, I was nervous. What was I going to say? What was I going to do? Would these men respect me? Would they laugh because Carmine and I were so young? Before that day, I thought that I was ready. When the day was finally in front of me, I wasn't so sure, but I had no choice but to face it.

"What's on your mind?" Carmine asked as I looked myself over in the full-length mirror.

"Just wondering how this meeting is going to go," I answered with a shrug.

"It's going to go exactly how you want it to go. You control this, no matter what other people think. You got this," he assured me.

I believed him and stepped out of the bedroom with Carmine behind me. Once we entered the living room, he took my hand and walked beside me. We were equal in all aspects, and we were entering the lion's den with an equal share.

I was surprised to see that no one had arrived yet.

"They are on their way. Get a drink," Capello ordered as he noticed the look on my face.

"I don't want a drink."

"Billie, trust me, have a drink. Hell, take two. You're a hothead and I don't want you to act up tonight," Capello insisted.

Instead of calling the maid over to fix a cocktail, I got up and walked to the bar to make two strong drinks for Carmine and myself. Once there, the doorbell rang and I froze for a few seconds. I was nervous about the meeting but tried my best to pull myself together. I had to go on as if I was self-assured. As I continued to make our drinks, the partners in the Pricey Pussy Empire started to spill through Capello's front door.

In all, there were only two besides Capello. I was shocked, thinking that there would be more.

As I placed the drinks on a tray, a man stepped behind me, got really close, and squeezed my ass. He then rested his chin on my right shoulder. "Make another one, will you?"

I quickly looked at Carmine, who was now on his feet, and I shook my head no. I ignored the man's request and headed over to Carmine. I stood in front of him and tried my best to get him to take his eyes off of the man who had insulted not only me, but him, too.

"Here you go, baby. Carmine, take the drink and have a seat. Do you hear me? Look at me." I watched as his nostrils flared and I prayed that my voice would calm him down.

"Marley, you have made a mistake. This is not a working girl; this is Billie."

I turned from Carmine, whose eyes were still on the man as he stood; and I watched for a reaction.

"*The* Billie?" the man asked as if he was disgusted. "She's a girl. A young girl at that. Are you fucking serious, Capello?"

I dropped the tray, emptied my glass, and prayed that it would stop me from cursing this man out.

"Yes, he's fucking serious," Carmine answered.

The air was so thick with hostility that I wasn't sure how we all got any air in our lungs.

"Okay, everyone, sit down. This is not necessary. Let's all have a drink and clear the air," Capello pleaded.

At first, no one moved; but, soon, as the maid came into the room with another round of drinks, we all took our seats.

"Marley, Dexter, this is Billie and Carmine. Billie, Carmine, these are the guys I call the brothers. I have already told you why they are here, so let's discuss things."

Before Marley let out a snide remark, I took the time to assess his brother, the other partner. He was a black man who dressed well, and was draped in diamonds. Nothing about him was understated. Everything on him was big, from his head down to his damn feet. He was not mouthy like the other and seemed to have some type of respect for the people who sat among him.

"These are fucking kids. Capello, are you fucking kidding me?"

I could feel my neck tightening as my pressure rose.

"Marley," Dexter snapped before continuing. "Let's hear what Capello has to say."

I watched as the man with the big mouth shriveled like a pussy after birth. I didn't know if it was because his size compared to Dexter, being that he was much smaller, or if it was the power within his voice. For all I knew it could be something I had yet to learn about the big man. Either way, Marley's mouth was shut.

"I am stepping away from this position. I guess you can say that my encounter with these two has changed me. My family has always been in the sex industry through porn and prostitution, so this is all I know."

"So why leave?" Dexter asked.

We waited as Capello stared off into space. "I guess I don't want this on my conscience when my last day on this earth appears. Sure, I will never be able to undo what has already been done, but we all have to wake up one day and choose to change. Our past is not who we are; our current position is what dictates who we will become."

"I just don't understand. What about all of the money you will be leaving behind?" Marley asked.

"How much money can one man have? Look around. We are sitting at the top, Marley. We have all become billionaires thanks to the agony we have caused others. No, money is not important enough for me to continue down this path. I have enough, and will never spend what I already have in this lifetime. I am done with this."

I listened intently to what Capello was saying. Wishing that his words would touch my heart, I really wanted them to affect me to the point where I wouldn't want his spot, but they didn't.

"So that brings me to Billie and Carmine. They will take my place, when they are ready of course. Bellissima will groom them, as she did me. And when they are ready, they will run things as I did. Right now, you can consider them silent partners until they are up to speed."

"But that little girl doesn't know how to run this business on this level. You have them sitting at the top of the food chain without a day of hard work. We all came from the bottom, and you're telling me that this little bitch is just going to be placed up here with us?"

I looked around the room for anything that I could use to teach this motherfucker a lesson. When I couldn't find anything, I picked up the bottle of liquor that sat on the table in front of us. Then I smashed it against the edge of the table. After taking a few quick steps, I was in Marley's face with the jagged edge of the bottle against his neck.

"You are not going to sit here and call me a bitch. I will slice your fucking neck open and worry about the consequences later, do you understand me?"

I waited for Marley to nod his head up and down before I continued with the bottle still at his neck.

"I don't need to know anything about running this business today because what I don't already know, I will learn. What I do know is what it feels like to be stolen and held captive. I know what it's like to have a sick fuck in your bed touching you when all you want to do is go back home to your mother. I know what it's like to have an old, dried-up bitch viciously hate you because her husband's hand can't stay out of your pussy. How about you? Do you know what that's like?" I asked, pushing the bottle into his neck until I saw blood. I didn't wait for an answer before continuing.

"I know what it's like to go to bed hungry, dirty, beaten, and mistreated. I know what it's like to be hopeless, empty, and lost. Have you ever had your little dick sold to old women for cash? Huh? Have you? So don't you fucking sit here and tell me that I don't know what it's like to be at the bottom 'cause, motherfucker, there is no lower than that. So you are either going to sit here and show Carmine and me some respect, or you are going to lose your fucking life today, do you fucking hear me?"

It wasn't until I felt Carmine's hand against my back that I realized that I was crying, and that he was behind me. I would never claim to be a killer, even after what happened at the Vega home, but that day I was ready to take Marley's life.

"You have anything else you want to say to her?" Carmine asked as I stared the asshole in the eyes. He shook his head no, but that wasn't enough for me. For a lasting reminder of the day he met Billie and Carmine, I took the bottle and slashed him across the right cheek.

As he screamed, I calmly walked back to my seat and asked the maid for another drink.

"Bravo, Billie. You have just earned my vote. My brother tends to treat women as if they don't deserve respect. I'm sure he has learned a lesson or two today," Dexter said, clapping his hands. I looked to Capello, and he sent me a nod of assurance.

"DeeDee, take Marley to the bathroom so he can clean up. Tell Silvia to come in and sew him up," Capello instructed.

Once he was out of the room, Capello and Dexter went over the details of the business with Carmine and me. By the end of that night, I was a full-fledged partner. I tried to call Zen once the meeting was over but, once again, it was too late.

Chapter 18

The Price of Evolving into Madam Blondie

The plane ride home was taking too long. I couldn't wait to see Zen's little face. Although her birthday was the next day, I had a feeling that at the stroke of midnight I was going to give her all of her gifts. I had missed a few celebrations of my birthday because of that evil bitch Mrs. Vega. Her husband would secretly celebrate with me by trying his best to please me. Maybe that was why I was so excited for Zen. Although she had already witnessed how ugly the world could be, I wanted her special day to bring her joy.

Upon landing in L.A., Capello told me that he would be at the house in the morning to explain to Bellissima the conversion of power. He was sure that she was going to raise hell, but in the end she had no choice. She had given her seat of power to Capello and, now, it would be passed on to me. We said our good-byes and entered separate vehicles.

"There isn't a day that goes by that I don't learn something new about you," Carmine said, taking my hand and kissing the back of it.

"And there isn't a day that passes that I don't fall deeper and deeper in love with you," I answered.

"I kind of missed Zen while we were gone," Carmine confessed.

I told him that I felt the same and we smiled at each other. The rest of the ride was spent in silence as I anticipated seeing our little girl.

I burst through the doors of the house and called out for Zen. "Zen, we're here," I shouted, rushing into her bedroom.

She wasn't in there, so I started to search for her. "Carmine, is she downstairs?" I asked from the top of the staircase.

"No. I can't find her," he answered.

Instantly, my heart started to pump faster with fear. Where was she, and why couldn't we find her? I ran to Bellissima's room. I found her on her bed with a book in her hand.

"Where the fuck is she?" I asked, getting straight to the point.

Bellissima slowly put her book down before lowering her glasses, and looking down her nose at me. "She is sleeping," she simply offered.

"Where the fuck is she?" I screamed as I felt myself losing control.

"She is in the room at the other end of the house. I tried to get her out, but she—"

I didn't care to hear the rest of her explanation. I just wanted to find Zen. I rushed to the far left of the house, and hurried to get the bedroom door open. Once inside, the sight before me caused me to scream, "Zen, what are you doing?"

Within seconds, Carmine was behind me, both of us in shock.

"She made me go with the man. I told her no, and that you told me that I wouldn't have to do dirty stuff like that, but she forced me, Mommy."

I could not breathe. The room was closing in on me as I looked in Zen's direction. She was stark naked, with the gun I had given her against her temple. I looked to Carmine to rescue me, to rescue Zen, but he was frozen in the spot he stood in.

"I told her no, Mommy, but she forced me. He touched me, and put his thing in my mouth. I didn't want to, I promise you. I told her that you and Daddy would be mad. Then he told me to smoke something, and that it would make me feel better, but it still hurt. It still hurt when he put his thing inside. Don't be mad, Daddy, don't be mad."

I was in tears, but they could not blind me to Zen's altered state. Her eyes were glossy as they moseyed around the room.

"Zen, baby, please listen to me. We are not mad at you. We love you and I need you to give me the gun." I tried to take a step toward her, but she screamed for me to stay away as she pressed the gun harder into her own head.

"Carmine, do something. Please help her!" I shouted.

"Zen, let me come close to you. I just want to help," Carmine pleaded. But as he tried, she started to scream again.

"He made me do dirty things to him, Daddy. Don't you understand? I am dirty now. I am ruined. Don't you remember, Mommy? You told me if I let boys touch me, I would be ruined."

It was then that I realized that Zen didn't see us, she saw her real parents, because I had never had that conversation with her. "Zen, give me the gun. Please."

"No, Mommy. I am a bad girl now. I am dirty now. I want to die." She started to fiddle with the gun. Her little fingers struggling to reach the trigger.

"Go, Carmine. Go get the gun," I screamed in a panic.

Carmine rushed in as I called out to a God I no longer believed in. But if He heard me that night at the buyers' circle, He had to hear my cries that night. Everything moved so slowly: Zen, Carmine, and the struggle to get the gun. The gunshot exploded throughout the house, and I was facing insanity.

I watched as Carmine fell to his knees. His back rose up and down as he struggled to take in air. I could not move, I could not breathe, and I just wanted to disappear.

I stood there clutching my chest, not knowing what horror I was about to face. Did Carmine reach her in time, or was he dealt the deadly blow of the bullet? It felt like a lifetime before I came face to face with the truth, the kind of truth that would haunt me for the rest of my life. How could this be real? How could I live without either of them?

The sound that escaped Carmine's body was bone-chilling, and I knew right then and there that it was Zen who had come upon an untimely death. Carmine rose to his feet, and faced me. I saw Zen's lifeless body lying in his arms. Her limbs hung without the spirit that had in some way started to heal Carmine and me.

Her face was gone, and her brain hung openly from her skull. I cried from the deepest and darkest places in me. We stood there, Carmine and me, once again hopeless, once again lost. We kissed the parts of her face and head that were still there. We cried openly and asked the gods above why. Why would they let this happen to our little Zen?

Soon Carmine would lay Zen on the bed, and we would be on the hunt for blood. I walked beyond the now locked door to Bellissima's room and headed for the kitchen. The house was littered with the help and soon-to-be sex workers asking what was going on. As I left the kitchen with the biggest knife I could find, I knocked the phone off the hook, and told them to disappear or I would personally kill each and every one of them. They hurried back to their rooms and left Carmine and me alone to deal with Bellissima.

"Kick the fucking door in," I demanded of Carmine.

"Leave this door alone'ah," Bellissima called out.

Her pleas fell on deaf ears. The closer Carmine got to kicking the door off the hinges, the more my heart leaped with indignation. I wanted her fucking head, and I was willing to do anything to get it. Zen was gone, and it was because of her. I did not care that taking Bellissima's life wouldn't bring her back, but as the God who didn't answer my prayers that night said, an eye for a fucking eye, and I was ready to take both of hers.

Once the door was kicked in, we found Bellissima on her bed with a gun pointed at us. She let off a few rounds, which caused us to retreat. Carmine went back to the room where Zen's body lay and he got the same gun she took her life with. Once he was back, I told him what to do: "Don't kill her; aim for her arm."

As bullets whizzed past us, I waited until I heard her scream from pain. Carmine took a look in the room and told me it was clear. When I looked in, Bellissima was trying her best to slide off the bed and reach the gun that had fallen on the floor. Carmine had blasted her in the arm and accidently shot her in the side of her belly. Because of her age and disability, getting out of the bed fast enough to retrieve her weapon just wasn't going to happen.

Strutting to her bed, I gave the old bitch a backhand across her frightened, wrinkled face. She flew backward on the bed only to have me yank her up by her hair. She screamed and pleaded but I ignored her. There was no mercy left in me as I tried to pull her off of the bed.

She fought as hard as she could. When Carmine stepped in to help after picking up Bellissima's gun, I asked him to take her to the bedroom with Zen's body. Once in there, he sat her on the chair across from the bed, in plain view of Zen.

"You can't'ah do this to me," Bellissima cried.

"You better sit there and shut the fuck up. I only need you to answer a few questions." My voice was surprisingly calm, although my body trembled with rage. "Why would you do this to her? I told you that she was never to work as a sex slave, didn't I?"

I watched as Bellissima ignored my question and tried to tend to her wounds. With anger filling my airways, I walked over to her and slammed the gun into the side of her head. "Answer my fucking question."

She yelled and grabbed her head as pain exploded on her face. "I had to. We got in a request'ah for a young girl'ah and she was the youngest in the house. Don't you understand? This is the business we are in."

"When did the request come in?"

Again, I waited for her to answer. When none came, I lifted the gun in the air to crack her in the head again, but her hand flew up. "Five days ago."

I froze as a chilling thought ran through my mind. "Did Capello know about this call? Was he in on this?"

The few seconds it took for her to answer felt like decades. "No, I didn't tell him'ah. The call'ah came in from another man."

"His name. I need the man's name." I wasn't asking. I was demanding.

She seemed to stammer before answering halfway. "I tell you the man who bought time with her, but not who made the request'ah. His name is Marcus Stanford. He's a doctor'ah."

I don't know what took over me, but I started to cry. If only we had taken her with us, this would have never happened. We were here, with her, yet we were unaware of this doom that loomed over her head. Then I started to think of all the times I could have called her while we were away, but I let it slip my mind until it was too late. What if she'd picked up the phone? Could she have told us about this? Could we have stopped it?

I was consumed with so much pain that I just couldn't talk anymore. I had tried to save Zen, but because of me she was dead. When I prayed to God, was I wrong? Should I have not asked for Him to let me leave with her? Was I the fate God was trying to rescue her from when Capello said he couldn't give her to me? Just when I thought I was doing something right, it turned out to be the biggest mistake of my life. Maybe it was better if I didn't care. Maybe it was better if I didn't have a heart. Was this the reason why Bellissima was the way she was? Could having a conscience be the death of you when it came to the industry of flesh for sale?

Carmine stood beside Bellissima with fire in his eyes. I had not looked at him since we were back in the room with Zen. I knew in his eyes I would find pain that I would never be able to take away, so I would rather not see it.

"Another dead baby, Billie. Another dead baby," Carmine started to chant over and over. I walked over to him and let him rest his head on my shoulder as I hugged him.

"I thought it was going to be hard to love her, Billie. I really did. At first, I felt nothing; but, now, I love her. But she's just another dead baby, Billie. Just like the one on the boat. I couldn't save the one I threw in the water, but I really tried this time. She made me love her, Billie. When I looked into her eyes, it was all real. All of the love she had inside of her, it gave me hope. Now she's gone. She's fucking gone."

With the rise of his voice came a brutal shove. I went flying into the dresser as Carmine seemed to black out. With insanity pumping through his blood, he turned to Bellissima and wrapped his hands around her neck. I climbed to my feet and ran over to him. I begged for him to let go, but I'm pretty sure he couldn't even hear me. He was no longer there. He was vacant, and all traces of him were gone. It wasn't until I said Zen's name that he loosened his grip.

"Zen wouldn't want you to do this. Carmine, please, let her go."

"I have to kill her, Billie. She took our baby from us."

As badly as I wanted him to kill her, I knew we had to come up with a plan first. "Please, let her go," I pleaded.

Under duress, Carmine let go of the old bitch. I stood there watching, almost regretting that I was allowing her to get some air. You would have thought that she would be grateful but, between long pulls of oxygen, I heard a few words slip from her lips.

"I . . . I told you. I told'ah you."

"What did you just say?" I asked in disbelief.

She held on to her neck as she tried to catch her breath and repeated herself. "I . . . told'ah . . . you."

She had my full attention now. "You told me what?" I asked with anticipation dripping from my question. I was close to her now, close enough to hear every word clearly. She glared into my eyes. I felt like I was looking death in the eyes. Her eyes were dark and hateful. The old me would have looked away, but the new me wasn't afraid.

"Go ahead, you old bitch. Tell me what it is you've told me."

Bleeding and unapologetic, Bellissima cracked a smile. "You know why you didn't let him kill'ah me? It is because you are not ready. You are not'ah ready."

That was it. I had reached my breaking point. She had insulted me for the last time. I held my hand high in the air and brought the knife down with force. Over and over again, I hacked into her flesh, trying my hardest to rid her soul of all its evil. The more I realized that I didn't have that power, the more I dug into her with my weapon. Her blood splattered around the room. Some landed on the walls, some on the carpet. As I screamed and plunged the knife into her chest, legs, and arms, her blood landed on me too. With each droplet that seemed to burn like acid against my skin, I felt as if her poison found its way into my soul.

The closer she got to death, the closer I got to becoming what she was. With each stab wound, I was becoming what I hated the most. I was becoming just like them. Just like the people who captured Carmine and me, the people who hurt us, and the woman who took our little Zen away.

I screamed and cried as I tried my best to kill Bellissima. I took all of my pain and anguish out on her. In that moment, to me, I was not only taking her life, but I was after all of the souls who harmed us in the past. She would pay for all their evil doing. By the time I stopped, she was still breathing, but I decided to watch her die. I wanted to be present to witness the taking of her last breath. I stood right there, right in front of her, with Carmine right beside me. Drenched in her blood, I looked up at the ceiling and spoke aloud.

"This one isn't for you, God. This one is for the devil."

A chill went through my body with the realization that I was leaving behind all that my mother had taught me. She always prayed, always believed that God would deliver her. When things were bad, she always spoke to the Man Upstairs and waited for a miracle. For me, in the middle of that room that night, I would forsake it all. Hope, fear, emotion, and God Himself would leave my heart and never find their way back in. There was no going back to la-la land. I knew the truth, and it wasn't pretty. There was nothing or no one who would perform miracles. There was no God to save us and keep us from harm. We were in this alone, so we would have to conform and come face to face with the fact that this world wasn't run by the gods. This dark underworld and even us, the depraved souls that roamed it all, belonged to the devil himself.

As Bellissima gargled on her own bodily fluid and clung to what little life she had left, she fought to reach the pen that sat on the desk beside her. With the pen in her hand and blood wetting the paper, she wrote her final words. I was too caught up in life leaving her body to care about what she was writing. Instead, I stood there calm and at ease.

Her life drained from her body while she was writing. I smiled as death approached and her eyes froze over with her last breath. Her head hung low. I looked at Carmine and told him to give me the phone. I didn't call Capello, but texted him and told him that he should come to the house tonight. When he texted back asking why, I simply told him that "she" was dead. He didn't ask any further questions.

"Carmine, can you bring Zen downstairs? I want to give her the birthday gifts we got her."

He went to the bed and proceeded to wrap Zen's body in the sheet that was on the bed.

"Don't cover what's left of her face," I instructed.

I didn't wait for an answer. I left the room and headed down the stairs. I sat on the marble floor in front of the front door and waited. When Carmine came down with Zen in his arms, he laid her on the floor in front of me. He went to the bags that were still at the door and brought them to me. First, I pulled out the teddy bear and showed it to her.

"See, Zen, I didn't forget. Here is the bear you asked for. It's almost as cute as you."

Then I showed her all the cute little dresses I bought for her. They would have been perfect on her. I liked the pink one the best. I knew that it was her favorite color. Lastly, I pulled out the necklaces. Carmine was on the floor next to me and looked on as I pulled hers out first.

"I got this for you because you turned out to be the missing parts of us, Zen. You filled the empty spaces in our hearts with your cute little smile. The way you would run to us and squeeze us as if you really missed us always made us feel wanted. It didn't matter if you were at your classes for just a few hours, or if you just went downstairs; you always came back and hugged us so hard that we always felt your love. We love you so much, Zen. We love you so much."

Next I pulled out the box that belonged to Carmine. "This is for you," I said, handing it to him.

He sat with the box in his hand as if he was afraid to open it. So I took it from him and opened it myself. I pulled out the necklace with the thick key and pulled him close so that I could place it around his neck.

"Without you, I am closed. You came into my life and became a savior from the moment I met you. You are the key to my existence. Without you, I am nothing, Carmine. I love you, do you hear me?"

Carmine hugged me as tears left his eyes. He told me he loved both me and Zen, and that he would always love us no matter what.

"This one is for me, Zen. Don't you think it's beautiful?" I asked as if she could hear me. "See, Carmine, it's all a set. I have the heart, with the insides missing, and Zen is the heart with a little keyhole for you to open. Without one, the other just wouldn't work. Now with Zen gone, her body won't be with us, but our hearts will always be with her."

It all made sense to me, and the jewelry symbolized what we all meant to each other. I would bury Zen with hers in the backyard, while Carmine's and mine would never leave our necks. We sat with Zen and waited for Capello to arrive. We spent that time telling Zen how much we loved her, and how much she would be missed.

"What in the fuck?" were Capello's first words as he walked through the front door. I wasn't sure if that was because of the sight of me covered in blood, or Zen's body being the first things to greet him.

"What happened, Billie? What happened to Zen?" DeeDee asked with tears in her eyes.

"She killed herself, so I killed Bellissima," I stated without hesitation.

I watched as DeeDee's eyes got big and she grabbed her chest.

"You fucking killed her? Shit, Billie, you are out of control. You can't fucking kill everyone off in this organization. Do you have a killing problem or something? Are you crazy? Is there something I need to know about your mental stability?" Capello asked.

I sprang to my feet and began to laugh. "Am I crazy? You shouldn't even have to ask. But since you want to know, I'll answer. Hell fucking yes, I'm crazy." I couldn't believe that he would think that I could ever be normal after all that I had been through.

"Well, what am I going to do with you? You killed everyone in the Vega house. You sliced my partner's face open, and now this. You can't fucking kill everyone, Billie, you just can't."

I looked into Capello's eyes and told him everything that happened in the house that night. I even told him that if Bellissima told me he had anything to do with what she did, I would have killed him, too. By the look on his face, he believed me.

"I had no idea that this would happen. Where is her body?" he asked.

When I told him where, he sent DeeDee upstairs to take a look.

"I told her that Zen was not to work. I made that very clear to her and I thought that she would be safe until you got back. I am very sorry."

"But why would she do this? Did she hate me that much?" I asked, trying to come to terms with things.

"That's just who Bellissima was. She did what she wanted and couldn't stand being told what she couldn't do. Honestly, I never thought that it would come to this," Capello answered as DeeDee came back downstairs. "Is she dead?" he asked DeeDee.

"It's just terrible up there. Yes, she's gone but, Billie, I think this is for you."

DeeDee held out a bloody piece of paper. I didn't want to take it but she told me that she thought I should read it. When I took it from her hands, at first I held it without looking at it.

"You took her life, Billie. It's only right you read what it says," DeeDee added.

When I flipped the paper, the words on it hit me like a runaway train.

You are ready now.

Capello took the paper from me and read it himself.

"But she always called me not ready. Why would she write this?"

Capello sat back in his seat and got comfortable before he answered my question. "A few days before we left, I had a conversation with her. We spoke about the new girls we picked up and how they were doing, and then we spoke about you. When I asked her what she thought of you she said something very interesting to me. She said that when you first came here, she saw no traces of a real boss in you."

"But something had to change her mind for her to leave this note," I spat with anger.

"Let me finish," Capello answered before continuing. "So, I asked her what she thought of you now. She thought for a while then told me that she had changed her mind. When I asked her why, she said it was in your eyes. She told me that the more she watched you, the more she saw darkness in you. She said that you were brave and that, sooner or later, you were going to take your position."

"What did she mean by that?" Carmine asked.

"She meant that Billie wasn't going to wait for Bellissima to hand her anything. Bellissima knew that this was going to happen. She told me that you would probably end up killing her, and that her death would be the only way she would truly know if you were the one to replace her. See, she killed the woman who ran this division before her and, now, you have killed her for it."

Capello had things all wrong. "I did not kill her for her spot. I killed her because of Zen. Bellissima is the reason why Zen is dead," I answered as I tried to prove my point.

Capello looked me dead in the eyes and opened them to the truth with just one simple question. "If that were the whole truth, why would you wait and kill her at the exact moment she told you that you were not ready? I know that you were upset about Zen but, you stopped Carmine from killing her over it. It wasn't until she uttered those words that you decided to end her life."

I wanted to convince myself that he didn't know what he was talking about. I couldn't answer him, so I sat quietly. His question would haunt me for the rest of my life, but you could only run from the truth for so long.

"Don't worry about it, Billie. Things always happen exactly as they were meant to. You are a hunter, and a hunter kills its prey for several different reasons, and hunger is always at the top of the list. I'm sure Zen was one of them," Capello said in a factual tone.

Still, I sat in silence. Some parts of me were angry at what he said, and the other parts were ashamed. Bellissima should have died for Zen and Zen only.

"Now, we have to get things in order. We will bury the bodies out back, call in the cleaners, and make a lot of calls. You wanted to be the boss, well, you have just paid the cost. Just make sure your account is full, Billie. This won't be the last time you'll suffer a loss."

I looked at Capello and asked him how much money this all was going to cost me.

"No, Billie, not money, Money will never bring back Zen. The loss I speak of is your heart and soul. This shit here . . ." he said, speaking of the Pricey Pussy Empire. Capello threw his hand up and pointed directly at me as he continued.

"This shit here is going to take all that you have inside. You need to make sure that the account that holds your soul is full; Carmine too. You two will need each other because you are stepping into hell, and the devil takes no prisoners. This is do or die and, as you can see, there will always be someone who is willing to kill just to take your place. Stay sharp, stay smart, and stay ready. This is your house now, so keep it tight. Welcome to your palace, Madam Blondie. You are home."

I looked at Capello and only had one request. "You can bury Zen in the back, but I don't want that rotten bitch here. Do what you want with her, just don't leave her here. And if you think that when I get her age, you'll bring a young girl in here to kill me too, just know that I'll kill her first, even if it's in her sleep. You say I killed for this position? Well, I am going to be in it until the day I die. If you thought anyone was the best before me, wait until you see how I run things. Remember, I am ready now."

The End . . . of What Was

Wilted Flowers Emerge

*Now That Destruction
Has Arrived
You have blossomed
Into what
Is Already Dead*

Chapter 19

The Price of White Powder

I'm not quite sure why but while the men were burying Zen in the backyard, and removing Bellissima's body from what was now my home, I headed to the old lady's bedroom. It was unintentional. It was as if my feet led me there without a single thought from my brain, and I put up no fight.

In her room, I just sat there. Thoughts of Capello's words rang loudly in my head. The need to be ready surpassed the grief of Zen's death and that was why I killed Bellissima. That was a frightening thought, but face to face with this terrifying truth it was as if I was ready. I was ready to step into what I had become. Long gone was sweet little Billie. Now I was Madam Blondie and I would live as the walking dead.

Sitting on the bed, I tried my best to fight the inevitable. Telling myself that maybe it was all in my head, I tried to convince myself that somewhere within me she was still there. That little girl who sat at the Haitian airport, scared and in need of her mother's warm arms around her, had to still be there. Her voice, soul, and everything about her were absent. I sat silently and listened, hoping that I would hear her distant cries. I waited to feel her heartbeat from within. I swear, I waited for what seemed like an eternity, but she was gone.

Enraged, I stood up and started to go through Bellissima's things as if I was looking for answers. I searched for clues that would lead me to whom I was sure to become. It was as if I was possessed with the ghost she left behind. I felt it following me as I moved around the room. I opened drawers, looked under the bed, and went through her closets. I needed an answer as to why this demon was chasing me. I had become manic, riffling through her things with blind fury. When I found nothing, I sat on her bed out of breath.

For a moment, reality hit, and I realized how crazy I was acting. I was in search of nothing, but I needed to find something to feel at ease. I sat silently, waiting once again, and this time the ghost of the madam before me led me to the nightstand. I opened the little drawer at the bottom and just stared at what awaited me.

At first, it made me think of Mr. Vega. I had seen him with the white powder before. There were nights that he would come to me with a little Baggie full of cocaine. He would sniff it and ask me to try it. I thought about it, but the one time I stuck my finger in it and tasted it, it made my mouth numb, and that scared me. Time after time, Mr. Vega would try to get me to take a sniff, but I always turned him down. However, that night in Bellissima's room, things would be different.

I picked up the black plate and admired the vast contrast the white substance held against it. I set it in my lap and, just as I had done the first night I had become acquainted with the drug, I stuck my finger in it and tasted it once more to make sure that it was in fact cocaine. Instantly, the numbing feeling made me smile. This was what I had been looking for. I needed something to make me emotionless. I didn't want to feel or be aware.

I wasn't sure how much I should be taking and, honestly, I didn't even give it a second thought. Picking up the plate, I brought the powder up to my nose, and lowered my face until I felt the cocaine against it. I plunged in and inhaled. It burned like hell and caused me to cough. I didn't know much about coke, but its harshness caused me to question its quality. Instantly, my heart started to race, and I was stuck. I wouldn't be able to move even if I wanted to. Everything seemed clearer and every little sound was heard. While sitting there I kept asking myself, *Is she there? Can I find her?*

I waited for her and, surely, she appeared. I could see her, the younger me, still innocent, still full of hope and fear. That day came to me as a film, flashing deep-rooted memories before me as if I was in the audience.

The short walk from the Toussaint Louverture International Airport in Port-au-Prince to the plane seemed to last forever. My legs trembled as I approached the big flying object that I had never been on. I was so afraid, and the only thing I wanted was to have my mother beside me holding my hand. I could see her hands so vividly, darkened from the coal she sold and hardened by life. I had witnessed people avoid touching them, as if her hand was too dirty to brush against theirs. For me, they were the most comforting things about her, and I missed them just as much as I missed her. My mother's presence always brought me comfort and the thought of not knowing when I would see her again scared me more than flying.

"Relax, Billie. Once we take off, I'm sure it will be a smooth ride," Mr. Vega said as he rubbed my back.

"My God, what a beautiful daughter you have. She is absolutely stunning," the woman in blue and white stated.

Mr. Vega smiled with pride. Before I could tell the woman who was checking our tickets that he was not my father, Mr. Vega answered her. "Thank you. She looks like my mother."

I turned to the man's wife, who didn't look too pleased with her husband's answer. Instead of being upset with him, she seemed to be mad at me as she rolled her eyes at me.

Once in our seats, I started to sweat. The space inside the plane felt as if it was closing in on me. Instantly, I changed my mind. I didn't want to leave the island of Haiti anymore.

"Take me back. I don't want to go. Please, sir, tell them to let me off," I cried, speaking in my native Creole while a full-fledged panic attack set in. Beads of sweat were running down my face and stinging my eyes, causing them to leak even more. I tugged at the seat belt that strapped me in place as horror crept in.

"Billie, I want you to look at me. We cannot take you back, honey. Please, I want you to calm down before they bring the police on here."

*Even while living in poverty, my mother
made sure that I took English lessons. Although
it wasn't my first language, I fully understood
the word "police." In my country of Haiti, there
was one thing you never wanted to be involved
with, and that was the law.*

*"Please, sir, no. I don't want police," I cried.
I tried my best to control my breathing as the
airplane door was pulled shut.*

*"Just give her a pill and shut her up," Mr. Vega's
wife chimed in. She had changed from the nice
lady with a beautiful, flowing dress to a mean
bitch who seemed to hate me for no reason.*

"No, no pill. I will be calm."

*Everything in me told me to scream and
holler, but fear forced me to sit quietly. Sure
my future looked bright, but it was that feeling
deep down in my gut that told me to scream
and demand they let me off that plane. But fate
and destiny don't work that way. What was
meant to be, good or bad, would always be.*

*The plane ride was horrible. My ears hurt
and felt as if they would explode. The very first
taste of American food I had was yogurt, and I
thought that the nice lady in the blue and white,
who had complimented me before, was trying
to poison me. It was the most disgusting thing I
had ever put in my mouth.*

It seemed like the longer we stayed in the sky, the more my ears hurt. I sat with tears rolling down my face while holding my ears.

"Here, beautiful. Try a stick of gum," Mr. Vega offered. I smiled at the kind man and took the gum, but it didn't work.

"Just lay your head on my shoulder and try to sleep. We will land soon and, when we do, the pain will all disappear."

I did what I was told and drifted off into a light slumber. When I woke up, we were landing in Miami, Florida.

I took in my first breath of American air and in my young mind it smelled of money, in a sweet way. Grow-ing up in Haiti, all I heard about was how rich everyone in America was and how that was the place to be if you really wanted to make it. I daydreamed about what it would be like when I made enough money to bring my mother here and what her first breath of America would smell like to her. I was already missing her terribly, but I knew that I had acquired a new purpose in life, and that was to work and provide her with a better life.

The ride to the Vegas' home was quiet. What stuck out in my mind was the texture of the leather seats I sat on. All my life, my only means of transportation was a camionette. A camio, *for short, is a pickup truck, which is transformed into a taxi with hard wooden benches. Anywhere from five to ten people would squeeze in the back hoping to make it to their destination on time. Coming from a hard bench, the butter soft seat under my behind was a dream to me. The car was spacious and fit for a queen.*

"This car, what is it?" I asked in my broken English.

"A Jaguar. Nice, isn't it?" Mr. Vega answered.

I sat in that vehicle and promised myself that I would buy the exact same car for my mother with the money I would make from modeling. That was the only thing that kept me going that whole trip. The dream of becoming a big-time fashion model would have to keep me going.

When we pulled up to the Vega home, I was amazed at the size and beauty of their house. My mother had worked as a maid in some nice places in Haiti, but none as beautiful as this. Upon entering the house, I gawked with pure excitement. The Vegas had taste, and I could only hope to be gifted with such exquisite taste.

"Carmine, take her shit downstairs," Mrs. Vega shouted.

That was the very first moment I laid eyes on him. He was tall, dark as night, and absolutely beautiful, in a manly way.

"Don't just stand there like a dummy. Move your ass," Mrs. Vega yelled.

Slowly, Carmine approached me. The minute our eyes met, I felt something. I wasn't sure what it was. We locked eyes and even as he reached down to grab my belongings, we never lost eye contact.

"Come with me," Carmine ordered, and I complied.

"What am I doing down here?" I asked as I surveyed my surroundings. The basement I was standing in frightened me to the point where I was shaking from head to toe.

"What in the fuck does it look like, white girl? You've been tricked, bamboozled, and misled."

I looked in the direction the voice was coming from as my mouth hung open. Her face and arms were covered with white bandages, making her look like a real-life mummy.

"What . . . what do you mean? Why I'm here? I come to model," I answered as fear riddled my Haitian-accented words.

"Listen to this one, she came here to model. Well, the only thing you'll be modeling is a fucking thong for the sicko who either buys you or rents you."

"Leave her alone, Erin. You could have let her sit down first," Carmine jumped in.

I started to back away from everyone until the wall behind me stopped me. This was a real-life nightmare, and I wanted to wake up. "I want Mr. Vega. Please, I should not be here."

Erin started to laugh, and the other girls joined her. "You are right where you're supposed to be, trust me," Erin added.

"Mr. Vega. Mr. Vega!" I yelled.

When the mummy started coming toward me, I panicked and headed for the stairs. I was halfway up the staircase when Mrs. Vega opened the door and came storming down.

"What in the hell is all the yelling about?" she asked before she saw me. Once her eyes landed on me, I saw anger in them as she marched me back to the middle of the basement. "Did you girls not tell her what was expected of her now?" Mrs. Vega asked.

"I tried to tell her but she freaked out," Erin answered as she laughed.

"Why I'm here? I come to model," I answered.

Without hesitation, Mrs. Vega lifted her right hand and slapped me. "Bitch, there is no modeling job. You're here to sell pussy. Do you understand me?"

I was in shock. What did she mean I was there to sell pussy? I called out for Mr. Vega, hoping that he would clear things up. He was the nicer of the two and it just came natural to me to call out for his help. When Mrs. Vega's hand slammed across my face once more, her violence came with a warning.

"Billie, stop calling out for help. My husband is nothing to you but the man who will sell your ass. You better calm down before I am forced to kill you. Do you understand me?"

I couldn't even answer. My head was spinning and I needed to sit down.

"What in the hell is going on down here? Why is Billie in the basement?" Mr. Vega asked as he ran down the stairs.

"Your new little bitch is down here acting a fool," Erin spat out with laughter.

Mr. Vega was now standing between Erin and me. He turned to her, and with one quick motion, he slapped her. Erin fell against the wall behind her. The white bandage on her face instantly became drenched with her blood.

"How many times do I have to tell you that you are not the fucking boss around here? Don't run that smart-ass mouth of yours until you are spoken to."

Instead of being upset with Mr. Vega, Erin sent a chilling look my way.

"Your wife say I'm here to sell pussy? I thought I come to model?" I looked at Mr. Vega for answers. I prayed that this was some big mix-up and I hung off of every word that slipped from his mouth.

"Billie, come upstairs with me. I will explain it all." Mr. Vega reached for my hand but I refused to give it to him.

"She doesn't need to go upstairs with you. Just tell her the truth right here and now. She is here to work as a fucking whore, that's it, that's all."

I fell to my knees and started to beg. For some reason, now that Mrs. Vega said the truth in front of her husband, I knew that she wasn't lying.

"Please, just send me home. I will tell no one. I want to go home," I said as I groveled at the couple's feet.

Mrs. Vega raised her right foot and swung it across my face. The pain was blinding and caused me to grab my head.

"Why would you do that? Come here, stupid bitch," Mr. Vega snarled.

Everything was out of control. Mr. Vega was physically attacking his wife as Carmine came over and helped me to my feet.

"I'm sorry, baby. I just thought that she should know the truth. I'm sorry," Mrs. Vega cried out.

Meanwhile, her husband was trying his best to put his size-twelve shoes up her ass. After *a few well-placed punches, and some kicks to different parts of her body, Mr. Vega pulled his wife close and spoke in her face. "Listen up, bitch. If you ever lay a hand on that girl again, I will fucking kill you. She is different, and she will be treated as such. She will be upstairs with us and she won't be sold until I say so, understand?"*

"But . . . but why? She's just another worker. That's what you said to me when I told you that I didn't want her to come with us. I knew that you liked her. I fucking told you that you wanted her."

Mr. Vega met his wife's accusation with another hard blow to the face. "You're fucking right I want her. She is mine, so that means you are to stay away from her. You want the truth, bitch? The truth is that the minute I saw her, my dick got hard. She is the most beautiful girl I have ever seen. The way she talks, the way she moves, her body, her smile, her eyes: they just do something to me. The truth is I fucking hate you! You have turned into an old, bitter bitch, and I can't stand you. What, did you forget that I found you at the auction block your damn self? That's why I fucking hate you. You left Colombia for a better life and got caught up in this shit just like these other girls, but you forgot where you came from. If I hadn't saved you, you would be a working girl just like the rest of them."

"You can't do this, baby. You can't have her," Mrs. Vega cried.

Pulling her close enough to smell his breath, Mr. Vega continued. "She is mine! I will have her upstairs and she will fulfill everything that you can no longer provide me with. I fell in love with Billie the minute I saw her and, now, she is mine."

I watched the woman who I thought held so much power fall to her feet and kiss her husband's shoes as she begged him to leave me in the basement. Just as she had done to me, Mr. Vega's foot met the side of her head, sending her body backward. It would take me years to understand Mrs. Vega's fears, and why she hated me. She was afraid that I would replace her as the girl her husband saved at auction. I would be the girl in his life she once was. I was also what she would never be again. Partly because of her age, but mostly because of who she had become. Her mean spirit and fleeting memory were her own worst enemies.

"Carmine, take Billie and her belongings upstairs. Get her settled in one of the spare bedrooms. Make sure she showers and is ready

*for dinner." Mr. Vega headed upstairs with his
wife following and pleading behind him.*

*While Carmine gathered my things to take
upstairs, Erin sent evil glances and harsh
words my way. "What did you do, suck his
dick? Why do you get to sleep upstairs while
we're down here? You're not even that cute. I
hope you fucking choke on his dick, bitch."*

*The other girls joined in on the laughter as
Carmine told her to shut her mouth.*

*"Mrs. Vega is going to kill you the first chance
she gets, if I don't get to you first. Stupid girl
made him hit me. You better watch your back,
bitch," she warned as I followed Carmine to the
guest bedroom.*

*Once on the main floor, I looked around and
eyed the front door. I took one look at Carmine
and realized that he was preoccupied with my
belongings. Sensing that this would be my only
chance to run, I bolted for the entrance. There
were a lot of locks, but I unlocked them pretty
quickly. Once the door was open, a loud alarm
went off, but I didn't let that stop me. I ran for
my life. All of the walking I had done in Haiti
had paid off and I was in shape for the escape. I
didn't know where I was or where I was going.
I just knew that I had to get out of there.*

I sprinted through backyards and, once a few blocks down, I noticed what looked like a police car from what I had seen in the American movies. I waved it down and asked the officer to help me. In my broken English, I managed to say that I was kidnapped and that I needed help.

"Okay, sweetie, come with me. I will keep you safe," he assured me.

I got in the back of his car and thanked God that I was able to escape the hell I was sure to face. As he drove, I closed my eyes and said a million thanks to the Almighty. I couldn't wait to be with my mother again. I just wanted to be with her and cry in her arms and tell her about this whole ordeal.

As I prayed, I felt the car come to a stop. When I opened my eyes, I looked at the house before me and screamed, "No, no, they are the bad people. Take me away."

The nice policeman smiled before he jumped out of the car and said, "I am one of the bad people too. Welcome back home."

He had to drag me back into that house kicking and screaming. I put up a good fight, but it just wasn't good enough. Once inside of the house, Mr. Vega thanked the officer and gave him a wad of money. As the officer walked to the door, I spat at his feet as a show of the utmost disrespect. He went to hit me but Mr. Vega stopped him.

"Don't worry, Jimmy. I'll take care of her."

"You better, she's a slick one. Beautiful, but slick," the cop added.

Once the officer left, Mr. Vega sat down beside me and lit a cigar. I stayed quiet in total fear that I was about to suffer a painful consequence for trying to escape.

"Billie, I understand that you are in shock but trying to run from this house can cost you your life. I know that we lied to you, but trust me when I tell you that being my special girl, well, that is as good as it will ever get."

When I didn't answer, he put his hand on my knee and began to rub it.

"Listen, we can't always have everything we want. I know that you would love to just go back home, but that's not going to happen. Just make the best of this and I promise you that it won't be so bad. You are mine now, and I will treat you the best, trust me."

He called Carmine over and told him to take me to my room. "Dinner is in an hour. Your clothes are laid out for you. Put on the lipstick and perfume I left on the bathroom counter after your shower."

I stood up without saying a single word to Mr. Vega. I followed Carmine without even looking back at him.

"Sorry to see you back," Carmine said, smiling.

"Sorry to come back," I answered.

"No one has ever tried that. It's like we all gave up the minute we walked in this house, but not you."

I looked at the handsome boy and smiled. "I never give up. One day, I leave and never come back," I promised in my broken English.

"I believe you. Trust me, I do."

"I want to go home. I just want my mom."

Carmine looked at me with pity in his eyes. Once I started to cry, he looked as if he didn't know what to do. I walked close to him and hugged him. I didn't know him, but he was the only one who had shown any kindness to me besides Mr. Vega.

"I just want my mom. I miss her."

"It will be okay. I will watch over you until you see your mommy again. It's okay."

I held on to him for a while and just cried. His words were comforting and I was thankful to have a newfound friend.

After sitting through an uncomfortable dinner with Mr. and Mrs. Vega, I asked to go back to my room. Mrs. Vega hadn't said much to me while we ate, but the way she looked at me let me know that she hated me.

"Go ahead, Billie. I will be in to see you in a little bit." Mr. Vega smiled.

I was having a hard time knowing how to deal with him. He was holding me captive, but was being so nice about it. Was it better to have Mr. Vega on my side and be his "special friend" and play nice? I just didn't know, and I was too tired to try to figure it out in that moment.

I got in the bed with the short dress Mr. Vega had laid out for me. I had wiped off the red lipstick he requested for me to wear and I prayed that, when I woke up the next morning, this day would be a bad dream. I was just starting to fall asleep when Mr. Vega entered my room.

"Billieeeee," he sung my name. "Wake up, baby. I have something for you." Mr. Vega waited for me to sit up before he held out a little Baggie toward me. "Sniff a little bit of this. I promise it will make you feel better."

I took the Baggie, stuck my finger in, and tasted it. "No, I don't want it."

At first, he tried to convince me to sniff the cocaine, but after a while he gave up. "Fine, maybe a drink will make you feel better."

I declined his offer, but he told me that he wasn't taking no for an answer. He left the room and quickly came back with a bottle of vodka. He poured the first shot and held it up to me. I took it, held my nose, and swallowed, almost on the verge of throwing up. The taste was revolting. I gagged a few times before handing him back the glass.

"That's a good girl. I want you to take five of them just like the first one, and you'll feel much better."

"I don't like it," I answered as I wiped my mouth with the back of my hand.

"Drink, Billie. Don't make me upset." His voice was stern and it scared me. He poured the shots, and I drank them all down.

I was starting to get hot and the room started to spin. Mr. Vega put on the television and sat in the chair beside the bed. As time went on, he gave me more liquor and I became drunk.

"You okay, Billie?" he asked as I lay back staring at the ceiling.

"I feel funny," I answered.

Mr. Vega stood up and sat down on the bed beside my right knee. "It's the alcohol, Billie. It feels good, doesn't it?"

I didn't answer. Instead, I closed my eyes to stop the room from moving.

"You are so beautiful," Mr. Vega said as I felt his hand on my thigh. I tried to push his hand away, but I had a hard time fighting him off. My body felt heavy, making it hard for me to move.

"The minute I saw you, I knew that I had to have you. I wanted to grab you and feel you right there on the street. I wasn't going to leave Haiti without you. That is why I had to trick you. I know you're mad but I just had to have you."

"Please, Mr. Vega, please leave me," I pleaded as his hand went farther up my thigh.

"I can't, Billie, I can't. Ever since I saw you, all I could do was think about you. I tried to tell myself that you're too young but I just can't help it. I fell in love with you as soon as I saw those beautiful blue eyes."

I continued to plead with him to leave me alone but he wasn't listening. When his hand reached the spot my mother always told me never to let a man touch, I tried to fight, I really did, but the vodka restricted my body's movements. He continued to rub me down there as he spoke.

"Just let me love you, Billie. Just let me love you. Don't fight me. I will make you feel good."

No matter what I said or tried, he would win that night. He did not penetrate me but his face did find its way between my legs. My body was now at war with my brain. What he did to me didn't feel bad, but I knew that it was wrong. It wasn't until a year later that I would find out the true meaning behind what he was doing.

On a talk show, the host had a special on molestation. She said that the predator at times tried to make what he was doing feel good in order to confuse you. It was a way to make you think that what was happening was your fault. It was a form of traumatic bonding. If he made you enjoy it, maybe you would grow positive feelings toward him and no longer see him as a threat.

I would blame myself for a very long time after that night. Even during the years of false love and knee deep within my Stockholm syndrome, I was blinded to the fact that, deep down inside, I truly hated this man. It didn't matter that by the age of fifteen, I considered what he was doing to me a form of love. Somewhere inside of me, I hated it and knew that it was all wrong. But with me blaming myself and physically growing to accept the abuse, it made him not only win the physical battle against me, but also the mental war.

The next morning, I woke up being dragged from my bed. "Get your ass out of that bed."

I tried to fight off Mrs. Vega but she had caught me off guard.

"You think you can spend the night with my husband and get away with it?" she asked as she continued to drag me by my hair.

I called out for Mr. Vega, but he never came to rescue me.

"He's away on business. No one can save you now."

She pulled and tugged on me until she had me down the first flight of stairs. Then she told me to stand up. While still holding on to my hair, she marched me to the basement stairs.

"This is where you will stay every time my husband leaves this house."

With a hard shove, she sent me flying down the basement staircase. If I hadn't grabbed on to the banister, I probably would have broken my neck. After rolling down a few steps, I caught my balance and walked down the rest. Standing at the door, she looked down at me and threatened me.

"If you ever tell my husband about this, I will not only kill you, but I will go back to Haiti and kill that dirty mother of yours."

I took her words seriously and never uttered a word about my temporary home to Mr. Vega.

I wasn't sure how long I had been down there before Erin started in on me. "Look who has come to play; it's the princess."

I ignored her, which caused her to come over to me. "You think you're special, don't you? You think that you are better than us because that sick fuck took a liking to you? Well, you're not. You are just like us. When they took you, they told you that you were coming here to be a model? That means you had it easy. Bitch. My very own father gave me to these people for drugs. They told him that they would use me as a blank canvas for a very special client who liked to scar women, and he didn't even care.

"Sofia over there, well, she's been doing this since they took her at the age of four. Can you imagine that? That is a baby, but they didn't care. And as far as the one in the corner, that's Terry. They took her right out of her front yard. Do you know what they did to her?" Erin asked as she poked me in the face. "They call her the throwaway. She's the one who men can buy to have unprotected sex with. She's had every disease in the book, even the ones you can't get rid of. They use her for the sick men, the men who are dying but still want to fuck unprotected."

I started to cry. I was horrified at the things Erin was saying. I couldn't help but wonder if these things would happen to me if I didn't comply with Mr. Vega and become his special girl.

"Save your fucking tears. We all have a chapter in the book of hell on earth; yours is just being written."

She walked away and left me dumbfounded. This just couldn't be my life. This was not what was in the cards for me. I made a decision right in that basement to do whatever Mr. Vega wanted. I also promised myself that being a victim of human trafficking would not be how my story would end.

When Carmine came down the stairs, I went to him and hugged him tightly. "I just want to go home and see my mommy. I just want to be with her," I cried in his arms.

"You will, Billie, you will."

"I just want my mommy, I just want my mommy. I just want my mommy."

"I just want my mommy. I just want my mommy."

"Billie, what is the matter with you? Billie, it's me, Carmine."

I was pulled back to reality by the sound of Carmine's voice. Tears streamed down my face and landed in the cocaine that sat in my lap.

"I heard you screaming about your mother, so I ran up here to check on you. What are you doing with this plate?" Carmine asked as he attempted to take the drugs away from me.

Again, I held the powder up to my nose and sniffed. I waited for the burning to go away before I quickly stood up. "Where's Capello? I need a meeting right away. Tell him to call the brothers. They must know that I am in charge now. I did it, Carmine. I felt her, I mean me, and she is still there. Tell him I need a meeting. Is he still here? Did they leave?" I was talking a mile a minute as I moved around the room. "Are they here? I'll tell him myself. Are they here?"

I didn't wait for Carmine to answer. I descended the stairs two at a time and found Capello out back.

"You have to tell them I need a meeting. I have to let them know that I am the boss now. I fought and killed my way to this spot. Call them now. I need to speak to the brothers."

Capello looked past me and asked Carmine what I was on.

"I found her in the room with Bellissima's drugs," he answered.

Capello shook his head and spoke to Carmine once more. "Everyone needs an escape, I guess.

I totally understand her taking a little sniff. I've been there a time or two, myself. Cocaine is a powerful drug, though. Make sure you watch her with that shit. It can go from a fun little habit to being a big fucking problem real quickly."

"Fuck the coke. I need a meeting. I need to speak to the brothers," I said rapidly.

"Okay, Billie, I will make the call. Just try to get some rest."

Rest was the last thing on my mind.

Chapter 20

The Price of Freedom

I had gotten six hours of sleep over the last forty-eight hours. Staying awake like that had me strung tight. I was wired, and the first thing I did was take care of my home. I had Carmine bring together all the working girls in the house; then I gave them a choice.

"I know that most of you here were taken from your homes and families. Now that I am in charge, I want nothing to do with kidnapping. If you're someone who was taken against your will, please stand up."

One by one, I watched most of them rise to their feet. I shook my head in disgust and asked them the question no one had bothered to ask. "I am giving all of you a choice. You can stay and work as a top-shelf escort, or you can go back to your normal lives with your families. If you would like to go home, please take one step forward."

Holding my breath, I waited. It seemed like no one wanted to take that extra step, so I continued speaking. "This is not a test. No harm will come to you if you choose to go home. Tickets will be bought with an untraceable credit card and you all will be free."

Again I waited. This time three of them stepped forward. There were two young girls, and a teenage boy.

"Come on, I am offering you a way out. There have to be more than three of you who want to go home."

I just couldn't understand what was happening. If I had been given the same choice, I would have been the first to stand and take that extra step. I would have given anything to be with my mother again. Looking at them in disbelief, I saw a girl slowly raise her hand, waiting for permission to speak.

"Madam Blondie, excuse what I am about to voice but my words are only the truth."

She waited patiently for me to acknowledge her request. I nodded and she continued speaking.

"We all would love to go back home, but . . . what will we tell our parents? Most of us have already served a client or two. We are already tainted. How could we ever go back home and face the people we love and tell them that we are now different? How can we tell them that we are not the same people who disappeared? How can we say that the person who is standing before them has changed into something they will no longer recognize?"

My heart ached while I listened. The words she spoke were true, and I also knew that I didn't have an answer for her. My situation was different. I had no one to go back home to, and no one to answer to. I was a motherless child who had no one to shame. My belief was that once you had no one to answer to, you could live your life as you wished, no matter the level of destruction. I walked close to her and, with all of the kindness I had left in me, I palmed her face with my hands and spoke.

"Sweetie, you could never erase what you have been through. It is now a part of you, almost a part of your DNA. It will mold you and change you in ways that you could never imagine. You may never recover from this, but you can heal. This life, it is like an open sore. You can pick at it and cause it to continuously bleed, or you can bandage it, medicate it, and let it heal. Go home if that is what you really want. By doing so, you could possibly restore everything that has been broken. It may mend your families' broken hearts, it may repair your soul. You will never know unless you try. I can't give you all of the answers, but what I do know is this world, the world you stand in right now, it will eat you up alive if you let it. Choose wisely, sweetie. This is an opportunity that was never offered to me. One that will never be on the table for grabs again." I stepped away from the beautiful Asian girl and asked the question once more. "Now, for the last time, who wants to go home?"

This time, all but three of them stepped forward.

"Go with Carmine. Give him all of your information and you will be home by tomorrow night."

I turned to exit the room but decided to leave them with parting words. "I know that you all have never left this house unless you were blindfolded. You will be leaving the same way. We can't take the risk of any of you getting loose lips. Remember how kind I was to you if the thought of going to the police ever crosses your mind. Someone will be watching you until you board your plane. As I said, remember this act of kindness, because if any of you ever speak of this house, or the people in it, I will hunt you down and kill you and every living relative you may have. This is not only a warning, but also a promise I intend on keeping."

I left the living area, headed up to Bellissima's room, and buried my face in the platter of cocaine.

"Billie, wake up. The transportation to the airport will be here soon," I heard Carmine call out.

I sat up in the bed with a splitting headache and a foul mood. "How long have I been sleeping?" I asked as I rubbed my temples.

"Fourteen hours. Are you okay? Maybe you should go easy on that shit," Carmine said as he picked up the plate of drugs and set it on the nightstand.

"Has Capello called?" I asked, ignoring his comment. I could tell that the answer was no, judging by Carmine's face, and that pissed me off. "The phone. I need the phone."

Carmine exited the room and returned with the cell phone Capello had given us. I dialed his number and waited impatiently for him to pick up. When he did, I offered no hello.

"Why hasn't the meeting been set up? I asked you for a meeting a few days ago. Yet, nothing has been put into motion."

"I tried to set one up for today but Marley said he wouldn't be able to make it. He said something about his kid being sick," Capello answered.

I threw my feet over the edge of the bed and stood up. "I don't give a shit about a sick kid. When I want a meeting, I should be able to get one. I can't stand that motherfucker. He thinks that he can just brush me off?"

I heard Capello take in a deep breath before answering. "I don't think he means any disrespect, Billie. Maybe he just wants to take care of his child. Maybe—"

"Maybe he just doesn't give a shit. You were there. You heard the way he spoke to me. Let me ask you this: if you had called the meeting, would he have shown up?" I asked, cutting Capello off.

Silence fell upon the phone line as I awaited an answer. When none came, I made a request. "I want his address." It was simple. If he wouldn't come to me, I would go to him.

"Do you think that's a good idea, Billie? You can't just show up at the man's house. That is stepping overboard."

I pulled the phone away from my ear and looked at it as if I was losing my mind. "Capello, I need that address. If having to step overboard means putting an end to the blatant disrespect, so be it."

"Why don't you try listening to logic? Showing up at this man's house will only anger him and cause him to lash out. You are going to fuck yourself in the long run if you don't change," Capello explained.

"I don't think so," I answered arrogantly.

"Oh, yeah? Well, I had a long talk with my father and uncle after what happened with Bellissima. At first, they told me that since I was the one who brought you in, I was going to have to deal with you. That was fine with me. Then, you killed a woman who has worked for us for years, and that got their attention."

"What exactly does having their attention mean, Capello?" What he said made me raise an eyebrow.

"It means that I have a warning for you. If you step out of line, Billie, you are going to have to deal with them. Trust me, that's not what you want to do. See, what you don't understand is you're new to this. You are young, and they don't know you. Everything you do is riding on my back, but here's the kicker: I won't be the one paying the consequences. If you were smart, you would stay in line and just deal with me. I'm the nice one. You are playing a dangerous game, Billie. If you're not careful, you won't last in this world too long, and you'll end up bringing Carmine down with you."

I understood where he was coming from, but my need to have a one-on-one with Marley outweighed the reality of Capello's warning. I took in a deep breath and laid it all out on the line.

"You are right, Capello. This is a very dangerous game, but I have come to play. I can't let this disrespect slide. You have been roaming this underworld for far too long not to know this. In this game, there are rules that must be followed, and there are also consequences once you break them, just like you have warned me about your uncle and father. If I don't take care of this now, how will the others know that I demand respect? I told that man to stay in line but he ignored my request. Now he must face the music, just like I may have to dance to mine when that time comes. I want his address, Capello. I have a pen when you are ready."

Capello knew that everything I said was the truth. In our world, if you let just one person get away with the tiniest infraction, word would spread and respect would be lost.

After thinking about it, Capello must have realized that I would not give in. He read off the address and instructions. He also told me that I could use his jet and yacht.

"By the way, most of the workers here are being set free. I want them replaced with willing participants," I demanded.

"I understand that you are feeling very powerful right now, Billie, but you don't bark orders at me. Now, ask nicely and I will see what I can do," Capello said into the phone sternly yet with laughter.

"I'm happy that you find this amusing, Capello."

"I am just amazed at your transformation. Usually, it takes people a little more time to get this hardened. With you, it almost happened overnight."

I was annoyed by his comment and let it be known. "You speak as if you knew me before this life killed everything beautiful about me. You don't know shit when it comes to me, believe me."

Capello and I sat silently for a short while until he spoke again. "I didn't need to know you before your kidnapping to know that this life that you have chosen for yourself, and also Zen's death, has done a number on you. You are not even the same girl who sat with me on the yacht. So much about you has changed in that short amount of time and, quite honestly, it's scary. If I could tell you one thing, that would be to hold on to a little bit of the old Billie. Don't lose yourself in the world of human trafficking."

Although I could have said so much, I ignored him and made one more request. "Don't tell Marley that I am on my way."

I hung up the phone before Capello could reply.

Chapter 21

The Price of Family Values

Once I got off the phone with Capello, Carmine asked me about the conversation.

"We are going to pay Marley a visit. We'll leave and head to the airport the same time as the workers. Capello's plane will be waiting for us."

"He didn't want to come to our meeting?" Carmine asked with a twisted face.

"I guess not. He told Capello that he had a sick kid at home but I think it's bullshit. We are going to go out there and teach that fucker a lesson. Are you with me?" I asked as I picked up the cocaine.

"I'm always with you, Billie. You don't ever have to ask. Get showered and dressed. We should be leaving in an hour or so."

Carmine waited for me to snort my drug of choice before giving me a long, wet kiss. "I love you, Billie Blue."

I looked into his eyes, smiled, and said, "I love you, baby. Always."

The flight from L.A. to Miami should have cooled me down, but all it did was give me too much time to think. I was driving myself crazy as I thought of how disrespectful Marley was to me on the day we met. I promised myself that I was not going to his home to hurt him. I was going there to set him straight. If things were to get out of hand, it would be because of him and not my temper.

When Capello gave me the address, he told me that if I wanted to get there unnoticed, I would have to also use his small boat. Marley's home was on the water and to avoid the gate that surrounded his estate, the easiest way would be to take a water transport. Once Carmine and I got to the marina, one of Capello's workers was waiting for us. Capello had already instructed him on everything that needed to be done, including disabling the security cameras Marley had in and outside of his home. When he told me that the cameras were off, I wondered if Capello knew that this meeting would end up in bloodshed and he wanted no proof of what led to it staying behind. He knew Marley better than I did. Did Capello know that he was going to be the same disrespectful pig he was when we first met? Did he know that I wouldn't be able to handle the situation without some things going wrong?

Once the captain of the boat alerted us that we were almost at our destination, I told him to let us off a house or two before, and to come back for us in an hour. Carmine instructed him to come looking for us if we weren't waiting at that exact location when he returned.

Once off the boat, Carmine and I made our way to the big, beautiful house on the water. We jumped the fence around the pool, and headed for the front door. We were acting as if this was just a normal visit.

"What's the plan?" Carmine asked.

"We are here to issue a warning. Try to stay cool. We both know that he's an asshole so just stay calm."

I rang the doorbell with Carmine by my side and waited. A beautiful Hispanic woman answered the door looking quite puzzled.

"Hi, we are here to have a meeting with your husband. Capello should have called ahead. Is he home?" I lied with a smile.

"Oh, you work for Capello? My husband didn't mention that he was expecting company," the woman answered, blocking the entryway with her body.

She held the door close against her body. I could tell in her stance that she didn't want to let us in. I wasn't about to explain myself any further so I pulled out my phone and dialed Capello. I told him the situation and, after, he asked to speak to Alexa, Marley's wife. After a few short minutes, she was all smiles as she opened her front door wider.

"Please, come in. My husband just stepped out, but he will be back soon. I did not know that there was a new partner in the company, and for you to be so young, my God," she said, sounding very impressed.

I smiled at how easy it was to gain entry into Marley's home. You would think that with the business he was in, his wife would have known better than to just let strangers in. I guess knowing Capello came in handy. She gave me back my phone before escorting us into the living room area of her home.

"Would you like something to drink? We have a great assortment of liquors. We haven't had much company since we had the baby."

Carmine and I accepted her offer. Alexa was very friendly. Her personality only added to her physical beauty.

"Where are you from?" I asked her while I looked her over.

She was stunning. Alexa had jet-black hair that hung below her ass. She was tall and thin, but in a healthy way. Her red clay-colored skin was paired beautifully against her dark features.

"I am from Mexico. What about you? You look exotic as well."

I smiled and told her that I was Haitian, and that Carmine was Cuban.

"That goes to show you, never judge a book by its cover. If I had to guess, I would have said that you two were the opposite. But that would be very ignorant to think that the darker person is Haitian."

We shared a laugh as she stood up to fix us a drink.

"You have a beautiful home. I couldn't help but notice the pictures as we walked in. You have a beautiful family as well."

Alexa beamed with pride as she walked back over with our cocktails. "Thank you so much. God has really blessed us with Junior. We tried for years, and it just wasn't working. After so many miscarriages, I had given up hope."

I could see the sadness in Alexa's eyes, but soon happiness would set in.

"Damn, I am so sorry to hear that," was all that I could offer.

"Thanks, but God came through for us. We lost five babies before Junior showed up and stuck around. I like to think of it as fate. Even when you can't understand why, God has His reasons."

I sat uncomfortably while she was speaking of God, but I tried my best not to let it show. In the background, I could hear the baby's wailing loudly on the baby monitor.

"He's been crying all day. This cold is really putting him through it," she said, getting up to check on her child.

"May I use your bathroom?" I asked as I stood up.

"Sure, down the hall, after the office on the right."

I told Carmine that I would return shortly and set off to find the bathroom. On my way there, I stuck my head in what I presumed was Marley's office and the first thing I noticed was the gun that sat openly on his desk. It was safe to say that his wife knew exactly what kind of business her husband was in. I continued to the bathroom and fed my growing habit with nose candy.

Carmine and I sat in the living room listening to Alexa and the baby. She tried singing to him, talking to him, and feeding him, but nothing worked. Sitting there, annoyed by the sound of the crying baby, the sound of the garage door opening caught my attention. That meant Marley was home, and I was ready for him.

I sat with a sly expression wondering what his face would look like once he saw Carmine and me sitting on his couch. I didn't have to wonder for too long. With a face full of shock, Marley asked what we were doing in his home.

"It's so nice to see you, Marley. You wouldn't come to us, so here we are, coming to you."

If looks could kill, both Carmine and I would have been dead.

"I don't like this shit one bit. I don't ever bring business to my fucking home. My wife and kid are here."

"Yes, I have met Alexa and she told me all about Junior," I said as I pretended to fix the gold and diamond watch that sat on my right wrist. I found it in Bellissima's room and had decided that it now belonged to me.

"What in the fuck are you doing here, Billie? What do you want?"

I smirked at his agitation before answering. He didn't scare me one bit. "I want my fucking meeting. Didn't Capello tell you that I needed to speak to you?"

I waited for an answer as Marley twisted his face in disbelief. "That shit could have waited. My son is sick."

I jumped to my feet and inched closer to him as I tried to keep my voice down. "I don't give a shit about your sick son. When I call a meeting, you better show the fuck up."

We stood there without another word between us until the doorbell rang. He walked away, opened the door, and greeted his guest. "Hey, Doc. My wife is upstairs with the baby, go on up," I heard Marley say.

Then, once the doctor was out of sight, he returned to the living room area. "What was so important that you had to come all the way to Miami and tell me?"

I took a sip of the drink his wife fixed for me before answering. "I'm here to tell you that I am the boss now. I am—"

"I know that already. You didn't have to come to my damn house to tell me that the old lady is training your little ass," Marley said as he cut me off.

I sat there for a few seconds just breathing. I didn't want to hurt the man in his own home. "You don't know a motherfucking thing. I killed the old bitch, which means that I am no longer being schooled, asshole. Like it or not, training day is over."

"You killed her? Are you fucking crazy? You're a stupid little bitch."

Carmine stood up, probably tired of his harsh tone and insults. The laughter that escaped my lips was deep-rooted and laced with pride and anger. "Yes, I am fucking crazy, Marley, but a stupid little bitch I am not."

Marley opened his mouth to respond, but the doctor who he had let in just a few moments ago came walking down the stairs and into the living room. "The baby is fine. He's fighting off a bad cold, but the medication I called in for him should work. Oh, excuse me, I didn't know you had company," the doctor said as he noticed Carmine and me.

"It's okay, Marcus. They won't be staying long," Marley said as he shot visual daggers at us.

"Well, I'm Dr. Stanford, nice to meet you. I'll give you my card just in case you ever need a great doctor," he said, and shook our hands.

I sat there trying to place his name. I knew that I had previously heard it from someone. I stared at the man wondering if I had seen him somewhere before. I noticed the scratch marks on his face before looking down at his card.

"Come into the kitchen and I'll make out a check," Marley told the doctor.

I watched them walk away, still needing to know how I knew the good doctor. "Did that man ever come to the Vega house?" I asked Carmine.

He thought for a few seconds before telling me that he didn't think so.

"I know that man from somewhere, Carmine. Think, baby. Have you ever seen him?"

Again, Carmine's answer was no. I stood up quietly and inched closer to the kitchen to get another look at him. Standing just a few feet away from the two men, I listened to their conversation.

"How did things go the other night? Was she all that you thought she would be? I told you that I only deal in the best pussy around," Marley said with a grin.

"Man, I had to fight that little bitch, had to knock her out just so I could really handle her the way I wanted. You see what she did to the side of my face? I had to make up a hell of a lie to my wife to get her off my back."

Both men laughed and continued with their conversation.

"I told the old lady that I would be back this week. I'll give her a call to set something up."

"Just go through me. I got word today that the old lady passed. Which one did you get? I may have to try her out," Marley asked his friend.

"She was some little girl from the islands. She was fresh off the boat. Ken? Jen? No, her name was Zen. She's a real pretty little thing."

I couldn't breathe. I looked down at the card in my hand and it hit me. All I could hear was Bellissima's words: *"I tell you the man who bought time with her, but not who made the request'ah. His name is Marcus Stanford. He's a doctor'ah."*

I barely made my way back to Carmine without having to cling to the wall closest to me.

"What's wrong?" he asked as I walked past him.

"I am going to kill them. I am going to kill them all. Stay here and make sure he doesn't leave. If they ask, say I'm in the restroom."

I made my way to the study with murder dominating my thoughts and emotions. Picking up the gun that sat on the desk, I made sure that it was loaded. I held the gun behind my back and headed back to my victims.

When I reentered the living room, both men sat talking to Carmine. Walking to the center of the room in a trancelike state, I stood before the men, playing God. That night, I would be judge and jury. I would be the deciding factor on who lived and died.

"Are you ready to leave now?" Marley asked, clearly annoyed that I was still in his home.

I ignored him and shot a question at his guest. "You spent time with Zen? My Zen?"

The doctor looked at Marley in bewilderment.

"Billie, I think it's time that you leave," Marley said as he stood up.

As Carmine got off the couch, I reached out and swung the butt of the gun at Marley's head. He cried out in pain as Carmine grabbed him from behind and wrapped his arm around his neck.

"Look, I am not involved in whatever it is you all have going on. I'll leave and you can sort it out," the doctor said as he stood up. I aimed the gun at his head and laid down the God's honest truth.

"You aren't leaving here alive, you sick fuck. You went all the way to L.A. to rape a kid? You're a fucking doctor. People trust you with their health and lives, yet you are going around molesting little girls?"

"It was my first time I swear. Please, don't kill me," the doctor pleaded.

"Your first time was one time too many. How could you do that? How could you do that to her? Do you know what happened once you left? She killed herself because of what you did."

Tears fell from my eyes. They were a mixture of sorrow and anger. My whole body trembled.

Not from fear, but from rage. I looked at Marley and had one question to ask. "Does your wife know that you sell little girls to sick motherfuckers like him? Before you answer me, know that if you lie to me, I am going to put a bullet in your child's head."

As blood dripped into Marley's right eye, he told the truth. "Yes, yes, she knows."

Turning my attention back to Dr. Stanford, I nudged him toward the intercom on the wall. Once he was standing in front of it, I told him what to say. "Tell Alexa to come downstairs, and bring the baby."

Marley tried to put up a fight, but Carmine had a strong hold on him. When he tried to scream, a few well-landed punches and Carmine's hand over his mouth stopped him. When the doctor didn't obey my command, I dealt him his own blow to the head.

"You have three seconds before I blow your fucking head off. Now tell her to come downstairs with the goddamn baby!"

He pushed the button on the intercom, while I glanced at Marley. He was squirming and a sinister smile crossed my face.

"I knew from the day we met that I would kill you," I snarled before turning my attention back to his friend. "One, two—"

"Okay, okay. I'll do it."

I watched as his finger pressed the intercom and the nursery button lit up. The doctor took in a few deep breaths before speaking. "Ahhh, Alexa, come downstairs."

I pressed the gun to his forehead and mouthed, "With the baby." Marley tried to scream and fight, but he would once again lose that second round.

"Please bring the baby with you, Alexa."

With the gun still pointed at his head, I pulled the doctor by his shirt collar and faced the living room entryway. We all stood there anticipating the arrival of Alexa and the miracle child. My heart raced and felt as if it sat in my throat. My veins pumped with adrenaline and my heart beat with revenge. Fate had dealt me a solid that night. Marley refusing to come to the meeting had put me right in that living room on the night Zen's violator would be present.

I could hear the clicking of her heels against the marble tile before she even appeared. The minute she turned the corner and her eyes fell on everyone in the living room, she let out a loud shriek. The bullet hit her forehead soon after. The baby was the first to hit the floor. The child's cries filled the air, and his mother's body fell immediately after.

"Do you see what you have done, Marley? I have killed your wife for Zen. I will kill all of you for her. Hold him in place, Carmine, don't let him go," I sang in an irrational tone.

Marley fought a good fight, but Carmine's youth and strength overpowered him. His tears and sorrow wouldn't change anything that night. The doctor was also in tears, but their watery eyes meant nothing to me.

"I am going to fucking kill you," Marley threatened as he managed to free his mouth from Carmine's hand for just a few seconds.

I laughed and taunted him with my words. "You won't be killing me tonight, but let me tell you what is about to happen. I am going to murder this asshole, and then I am going to kill you."

"What about my baby? Please don't hurt Junior," Marley cried.

"You took away my baby and you think that I am going to let yours live? Everyone will die including your offspring."

With my revelation, Marley fell to his knees.

"The baby, at least pick up the baby. We are paying for what we did, but please don't hurt an innocent child," the doctor begged.

I turned him around and looked him dead in his eyes. I wanted him to see the evil that dwelled within me because of people like him. "Fuck that baby. You didn't give a shit about the baby you traveled to L.A. to fuck. Get on your knees."

I had grown numb to all of the begging and pleading. Because of those two men, my Zen was gone. There was nothing they could have said that would save them. With baby Junior's voice adding the melodic backdrop to the mayhem at play, I looked dead into the doctor's eyes and started to scream. There were no words, just madness and anguish. My continuous shouting caused the doctor to panic.

"Please stop yelling. I am so sorry, please, just stop."

As he approached me in what looked like an attempt to calm me down, the thought of him touching me filled me with disgust. I squeezed off a round and watched as the bullet caught him in the chest. The doctor stumbled backward before hitting his back against the wall. I walked close to him, needing to be so close to his death that I would feel it.

"It is because of people like you that I was even born. They raped my mother and, through that cruelty, I was conceived. Then the Vegas took me and I had to endure night after night of molestation. You people will never understand what we become after you touch us and slaughter everything good in us. I have spent years carrying the blame, telling myself that I was despicable because I allowed it to happen. I even made myself believe that this man loved me, and that I loved him too. I didn't even realize until now that, just like my mother, I too was just a victim. You are a fucking lowlife who likes to prey on young girls and destroy them. You killed that beautiful little girl way before she put that gun to her own head and pulled the trigger. You took her soul from her and just left an empty shell. I fucking hate you and every child-molesting sick fuck like you. If there is a hell, I hope you fucking rot."

Pain clung to my words as clarity wrapped me in its arms. Right there, in the middle of that room, it hit me that I was a victim. I realized that I was not to blame for what someone else chose to do to me. It was freeing yet left me with so many questions. While standing there watching the doctor bleed, I questioned the depth of my mental instability because of what was done to me. But just as soon as the question showed up, it disappeared as I pushed on to finish the task at hand. There was no need for any more words. I pulled the trigger once more and ended the doctor's life.

"Come on, Billie, let's finish the job," Carmine urged.

I had been standing in front of the doctor's dead body admiring his lifeless frame as if time was standing still. I silently spoke to Zen and told her that this was all for her. I told her that, by the time I left the house, she would be able to rest easy knowing that I had avenged her death.

After my short conversation with her, I turned to Carmine and the weeping Marley. "I'll be back," I said to Carmine, and headed up the stairs.

I searched the upper floor for Marley's bedroom. Once I located the master suite, I made my way to the closet and pulled out a short-sleeved polo shirt. While exiting the room, I stopped and took a few long seconds to look at myself in the floor-length mirror. I tried to see the old me in the reflection staring back at me but, once again, she was absent. I reached into my pocket for the little Baggie of white powder, stuck my face in it, sniffed, and went downstairs.

Before I went back into the living room, I stopped in the kitchen and picked up the biggest knife Marley's home had to offer. I wanted to kill him personally. I didn't want to stand from afar and shoot; that would have been too easy. Just like I had done with Bellissima, I needed to feel his blood against my fingers.

When I entered the living room, Marley was pleading with Carmine. He offered him money, drugs, and jewels, but that only enraged Carmine.

"Motherfucker, that shit doesn't mean anything to me. You and your friend killed Zen and, unless you can bring her back, you're a dead man," Carmine barked as he kicked Marley in the back.

I halfway ignored their conversation as I undressed. Once I stood in only my undergarments, I put on the polo shirt. I walked over to the now silent child and picked him up by one arm. I stood with the baby in my left hand as the knife hung from my right.

"Hey, Marley, look what I got."

The minute Marley turned to face me he let out a harrowing cry. "Billie. Please, I beg you, take my life, but don't hurt my boy."

I swung the baby violently in the air, and brought him back down. This time, Carmine spoke up. "Billie, don't do that. We did not come here for that."

My eyes squinted in anger. How dare he feel sorry for Marley's brat? This was about revenge for Zen, and we needed to be on the same page. "I don't give a shit about this fucking baby, Carmine. Hey, Marley, watch this," I said, holding the baby to my chest, and putting the knife against his neck.

Carmine took one step forward. It seemed as if he was prepared to let go of Marley to save the baby boy. "Billie, I need you to listen to me. You cannot hurt the kid. Just put him down and let's deal with him," Carmine said, pointing at Marley.

With pure anger and disregard for the baby, I threw him on the couch without even looking in that direction. He started crying again, and that only served to push me further into a state of total madness.

I leaped toward Marley as if I was in a video game, and brought the knife down into the middle of his frightened mug. Then I stabbed his flesh over and over again. All the while, I was screaming Zen's name, telling her that this was all for her. Soon, Carmine would back away. I heard him begging me to stop, but it was the same way with Bellissima. I just couldn't cease and disconnect myself from the chaos I revered. I wanted to make minced meat of him and I would stand there and try my very best.

"Billie, you have to stop. We have to get out of here," a foreign voice called out. When I looked up, it was the man from the boat.

Even after his request, I hacked into Marley's body with the same force as the first slash. I was still angry. I was still too hurt to just walk away.

"Oh my God, she has gone crazy. You have to stop her," I heard the man say to Carmine.

As he headed my way, I told Carmine to stay away; but he didn't listen. He came from behind and tried to get the knife out of my hand, but I swung it out of his reach. He tried to pull me away, but I clung to Marley's body, dragging it as I continued to slice and dice. Finally, the man from the boat pulled on the dead man's body, and Carmine was on the other end pulling me away. That was the only way the two men were able to get me to stop stabbing at Marley's body that night.

In the bathroom, Carmine helped me clean up. I was there, but on the inside I felt vacant. I felt like I was outside of my body watching a dark and moody film. I refused to speak to Carmine, still upset with him about the baby. He tried to make small talk, but I was not giving in.

Once back in my own clothes, we went to the living room where there was now a crew of men.

"You two get out of here. My guys will clean the house and check for security cameras. Throw that shirt you had on into the ocean and the salt water should clear it of any blood. When you get home, take everything off. That means your shoes, and even your underwear. Bag it up and wait for the guys to pick it up. I'll call Capello and let him know when things are all clear on my end. Harry will take you back to the airport," the man who brought us to the house instructed.

"What about the baby?" one of the other men asked.

I looked at Carmine, he looked at me, and I knew exactly what he was about to say.

"We'll take it with us."

I stopped dead in my tracks and spoke for the first time since killing Marley. "It doesn't matter if you let me do it here, or at our own home. That baby won't live to see the next twenty-four hours."

With that, I turned my back on the blood-drenched house, the men at work, the baby, and Carmine too. I walked to the boat with him and Junior in tow, and threw the shirt in the water as instructed. I wouldn't speak to Carmine again until we were home, sitting in Bellissima's bedroom. The baby would be on the lounge chair, and I would have a gun in hand.

Chapter 22

Carmine

The Price of Loving Billie Blue

The first thing I did once we got on the boat was check the baby out. I wanted to look for any noticeable physical injuries since he had fallen out of his mother's arms and, afterward, was manhandled by Billie. He seemed okay, besides the bad cough, but I would call a doctor to the house the minute we landed.

Throughout the flight, I kept looking over at Billie, trying to recognize the woman who sat across from me. Sure, we both had changed from our days in the Vega home, but I had never met the monster who stood in front of me at Marley's place. That thing, that evil, it was far beyond anything immoral I had ever experienced while with her. All along I thought that I was the dark soul between us, and although in some ways I still was, Billie's spirit that night surpassed the gloom I housed within.

I didn't know what would become of us, but the one thing I knew was that I wasn't going to let her kill the baby. How many children had to die for her to realize that it was wrong? I was just as upset as she was, but this infant didn't choose this life or his parents. As I held him in my arms, all I could do was think about that baby on the banana boat I couldn't save while on my trip to America; and, this time, I wasn't going to let go.

The ride home was a cold one. However, it wasn't due to the weather. The chilly atmosphere was all because of Billie's cold-as-ice attitude. I was learning to leave her alone when she descended into those melancholy moods. I figured that it was better to let her come out of it than to fight.

As we rode in the car, Junior's cough sounded horrible. I called Capello and asked him to send a doctor to the house immediately. When he asked about the events at Marley's home, I answered that I would tell him in person.

I sat in the living room with Junior and waited for the doctor. Now that we were home, my heart raced with anticipation. I knew that Billie hadn't changed her mind about killing the boy and I hadn't changed mine either. What bothered me was the lingering question that nagged me. If it came to Billie or the baby, where would my loyalty fall? Of course I loved Billie. I would even die for her, but there had to be a line that neither of us should ever cross.

Looking down at the sleeping child, I knew I wouldn't be able to make a decision at that moment. Or maybe I was afraid of the answer I already had. Billie would just have to understand. Just as she instantly felt the need to protect Zen, that was how I felt about the baby in my arms.

The doctor prescribed cold medicine for the infant and told me that he had no fever. I was told to bring the child to his office in three days and I agreed. I couldn't help but wonder if Junior would even make it to see the weekend, but I kept that thought to myself.

Once he left, I knew that it was time to get things straightened out with Billie. She had not left Bellissima's old room since we arrived. I could only imagine how much coke she had sniffed in the two hours we had been home and I prayed she wasn't zonked out of her mind. I thought about leaving the baby in our room as I went to go speak to her, but I prayed that the sight of him would change her mind about hurting him. So I brought the kid along.

I stood in front of the bedroom door asking myself if I was ready for this conversation. I was afraid of the possibility of walking out of that room without the person I loved most in the world. I could never imagine hurting Billie. The thought alone gave me chills; but no more babies. I couldn't let another child die without intervening.

"Billie, we need to talk," I said, entering the bedroom.

She looked up from the platter of drugs, using her finger to wipe her nostril. Then she glanced at me after completely cleaning her nose. "Carmine, if it's about that fucking baby, I don't want to hear it." Her tone was still icy.

I shook my head in disbelief as I sat down at the foot of the bed. "It is about the baby and we need to talk about this now."

I watched as she rolled her eyes at me and lowered her head to do another line. She snorted up the powder before brushing me off once more. "There is nothing to talk about. That baby is already dead to me."

Rage seeped into my pores and flew out of my mouth. "How dare you say that shit to me?" I asked, and leaned forward and smacked the plate out of her lap. I continued as her eyes sat on the drugs that were now on the floor.

"You are so fucking coked out that you're not thinking straight. What would make you think that I would let you hurt this kid? Don't you remember what happened to me? I am still the same Carmine who would damn near cry to you about my past."

Billie stood up and threw her hands on her hips. "Why would you do that? Why would you throw my shit on the floor?" she asked, speaking of the drugs.

It angered me that she wasn't even listening to me. "I don't give a fuck about that. I am talking to you about this baby," I voiced while standing up.

Who was this person who stood before me? There was no resemblance to the Billie I once knew. When she turned her back on me, she mumbled hurtful words as she looked through the nightstand for more of Bellissima's drugs. I put the baby down on the bed and walked closer to her. I grabbed her arm and yanked her toward me. I got in her face and tried to make her understand my feelings.

"What have you become, huh? It was one thing to kill the people at my aunt's house, and it was even understandable to avenge Zen's death, but this? That is an innocent baby. He had no choice in what his father did to Zen or what his mother knew. He is just like us. We were forced into the situation we escaped, just as he was born to his shitty parents. Billie, you have to wake up and realize that this is wrong."

Billie looked into my eyes and, where I had once seen the world, I saw nothing. "I fucking hate that baby, Carmine. Do you hear me? I hate him because while he is in the world, there is a chance that he may become just as fucked up as us. Why are you trying to save him? Didn't you see what happened once I intervened in Zen's life? She's gone, Carmine. She's gone."

Her words ripped me in half and, for the first time since walking into our home that night, my heart beat for her again. My grip on her arm softened and my soul bled for her.

"Billie, baby, it's not that I don't understand what you're feeling. I just can't have another dead child's soul as a burden to carry. I may have killed that kid on that boat but, that night, I died too. I can still hear that baby's cries, and I can still see the mother's eyes. Don't you understand, Billie? There is no coming back from this if you kill that baby. I already fear what you have become. I don't think I will be able to love what you will transform into if you do this."

The look on her face told me that my words had penetrated her deeply. I tried to stop those words from leaving my mouth, but the truth has a funny way of ripping free from the lies that bind and showing itself even when you try to suppress it.

Billie's face turned sour as she inched closer to me. The intensity in her eyes made me uncomfortable, as the daggers she shot at me was something I had never experienced from her before. "You stand here telling me that you are not sure if you will be able to love *me?* It's not you who cannot recognize me; it is you who stands here as somebody new. I am still the Billie who cheered you on as you killed every living soul at the Vega house. I am still the same girl who marched into Capello's home not knowing or caring if I would die. I am Billie Blue Blondie, the one who walked into Marley's house and killed the people who wronged not only us, but Zen as well. How dare I? No, how dare *you?*"

I stood silently as her words washed over me. As much as I hated to believe it, most of what she said was true. "Yes, you are mostly right, but do you know why it is so hard for me to accept this? It is because you have grown into this monster right in front of my eyes and I didn't even notice it. Slowly, you shed your old skin; and, look at you now. Although it was a fast transformation, you morphed into this creature that I was trying to avoid becoming myself. Billie, I love you, I swear I do, but wrong is wrong. We got our revenge. Now, let's give this baby the future that was robbed from Zen. I am not asking for the girl who walked out of the Vega home; I want the girl who walked in."

Billie started to cry. I could tell that she was at battle with herself. I begged her to please see things my way. I silently prayed to God to touch her heart, but it just didn't work.

"Carmine, I would never ask you to kill him. I know your history with children and what it has done to you. But I need you to understand that Junior has their blood running through his veins. He is a part of what they were and will always be a constant reminder of what we lost. Children have been placed on this earth to suffer, just like us. Can't you see that? They are weak and so vulnerable to the same kind of vultures that preyed on us. That is why I will do it myself. No matter what you say, I am killing that baby tonight."

With her last statement, I had given up hope in thinking that my words would change her mind. I grabbed her by both arms and roared in her face. I told her over and over again that this was wrong. Soon, I found myself savagely shaking her. I was losing control and had to take a step back. I wasn't sure if it was the drugs, or if this was really her. I figured that there was only one way to find out. I looked down at Junior as he awoke from his nap and I picked him up. I sat him on the lounge chair and returned my attention to Billie.

"I am going to leave him here and go to our room. Billie, if you kill this baby, I am not sure what will become of us. I want you to think about the love I have for you, and the love you have for me. If killing this kid is worth losing that, well, I guess we'll have to find out what happens to us from there."

I didn't wait for her to answer. My feet felt as heavy as cement blocks as I headed for the bedroom door. I didn't want to leave the child behind, but this was the only way I would ever be able to see with clear eyes who Billie was.

Everything in that room echoed as I awaited Billie's decision. The clock seemed to tick loudly, but it still felt as if time was standing still. The longer I waited, the darker my thoughts sank. For the first time in my short life, I thought of killing Billie. The words I spoke to her were true. I would not be able to find it in myself to love her if she harmed Junior.

How could I love her as I did before if this were to happen? Killing the baby would show me that her love was an illusion. The way I felt was if you love someone, you don't do what would hurt them the most. She was the only person walking the earth who knew what happened to me on that boat. If she could just bypass the devastation of that night and its effects on me, I would have to bypass the love I had for her.

I started to pace the room. Facing the thought of not having her in my life made me nauseated. What was I thinking? Could I really do it? I loved her and only lived for her. I had to sit down as I became dizzy with confusion. I started to feel guilty, turning against my own beliefs. The thought of Billie and Junior in the same room was driving me insane. I had to wait and see what happened because killing her just couldn't be done. Not by me at least. Could I hire someone to do it if she actually went through with her distorted plan? I didn't know. One minute I wanted her dead; the minute after that I would curse myself for even having such thoughts.

I had just taken a seat on the bed when I heard it. The sound of gunfire hit me as if it was the bullet. I screamed out in horror. She had done it. She killed the baby knowing that things would change between us. How could she? I got off the bed and went to the dresser with tears streaming down my face. I took out Zen's gun and sat on the chair. I was left with no choice. I would wait for her to come to the room and do the unthinkable; but, I still didn't know what that was. Was I going to kill her, or turn the gun on myself?

After mulling over the situation, I realized that there was only one thing left to do. So I waited for her. I knew Billie would eventually have to come to the room. I was at the end of my rope. I would go from feeling nothing at all to feeling everything at once. I heaved for air, unable to control my breathing. I hated and loved her all at once and the inconsistencies I felt within had dragged me to the brink of insanity. Emotional overdrive had set in and I tried my best to hold on until she appeared. In the meantime, I just had one question, which I would ask aloud over and over again to myself: "Why, Billie, why?"

The sound of her shoes announced her arrival as she stood behind the bedroom door. By then, I had numbed myself with liquor. I tightened my grip on the gun and held my breath. I would pull the trigger the second she walked in the door. I wanted her to realize that her choices in life wouldn't only kill Zen or the baby but, if she made the wrong ones, they would kill what we had, too. With that thought, I recognized where I had put the blame. Secretly, I held her partially liable for Zen's death, and that sickened me. She was not to blame, and in my anger I had allowed my heart to stroll down the street of misplaced liability. Billie was only trying to save her. The same way I wanted to save Junior. Where she had failed, it was hard to swallow the fact that I had done the same. Our botched attempts to save these kids were unsuccessful. Although we tried, our efforts just weren't good enough.

Hearing the door creak open, my heart raced. Unsure of my plans, I asked myself if I was really ready to kill her, or die. The moment she stepped into the room, I took in a deep breath. Everything changed that quick, in a second. I looked at the girl I loved with every morsel of my being and accepted the reality of our situation. Everything would be different from that moment. The lies I filled my head with demolished the truth that was once between us, and that was sickening to me. Nothing was more hurtful than looking her dead in her eyes, and coming to terms with what stared back at me. The death of what we were, and the dying certainty of our love, would come back to avenge its victim in the future. And whoever that victim was, they wouldn't even see it coming. That was always the consequence of murdering pure love and, that day, we both would have blood dripping from our fingertips.

Chapter 23

The Price of the Journey

The room had somehow become smaller once Carmine walked out of it. I tried my best to shake his words from my brain and heart, but they clung to every inch of my soul. How could he not love me? That thought felt foreign to everything I had always known.

I looked at the pile of white powder on the floor and questioned my emotions. Was I wrong for wanting to get rid of this baby? No, there was no way. All I could do was think of Zen and what they had done to her. What about what they had done to Carmine and me? The agony from Zen's absence would forever linger and cause a pain so deep that words would never do it justice. She was a chance for me to right the wrongs that had been done to me. Through her, I would get back my childhood while watching as she live hers. She had become a part of me, and I her. She was the person who had disappeared. She was the second coming of me.

I picked up the gun and walked over to the baby. He was sitting up and smiled once I approached him. Eyeing the drugs Carmine flung to the ground, I wished that I had just one more sniff available. I raised the gun to the baby's head and closed my eyes. As I stood there with a sturdy hand, I asked God to welcome this baby home with open arms.

God, it's Billie. I'm not sure if you've been watching, but if what my mother told me in the past about you knowing everything we do is true, I'm sure that you are ashamed of what I've become. But if that's the case, God, where have you been? Why would you let things go this far? I know that we are born with our own free will, but every action is followed by a reaction. Why didn't you save us when you had the chance? Instead, you let things linger until our hands became stained with blood. Now what, God? Now what? I don't know. My mother always said that I should never question you, but it seems as if the devil has been working a little harder than you these days.

Anyway, I just wanted to ask you to please watch over this baby. Deep down, I know that Carmine is right when he says that this child is innocent, but, I just . . . I just . . . I just can't let what happened to Zen happen to him. God, if you are listening to me, please step in this time and make sure to save this baby's soul.

That was it. Now, all I had to do was pull the trigger. Breathing heavily, as beads of sweat formed against my forehead, I did it. I pulled the trigger, but nothing happened. I had forgotten to take off the safety. As I tried to right my mistake, Junior caught my eye and I could not turn away. Even as I removed the safety, he smiled and played with the muzzle of the gun. I was stunned. Not at his actions but because, for the very first time that night, I had seen something in the baby that I had never seen before. There was a light in his eyes as he began to laugh and reach for me to pick him up. No, this couldn't be happening. Were my eyes playing tricks on me? I stood there, astounded by what sat before me. This child, who I had considered dead, came alive. He giggled and asked for me to pick him up, using body language in the form of outstretched arms.

I thought that maybe I was still high and the drugs had me seeing things, but it all seemed so real. I lowered the gun and picked up the laughing baby. Now in my arms, he looked into my eyes and smiled so deeply it was as if this was the happiest moment in his short life. His hands played with my face as tears formed and fell from my eyes.

"God, is this you?" I asked aloud.

The infant laughed with glee, which caused me to giggle along. I held Junior in my arms and asked him for forgiveness. That little boy had God in him. Although I had my own issues with the Almighty, my mother's voice danced in my heart. I knew there was a God and, although at times I felt as if He had forsaken me, through baby Junior I knew that He was present.

In my haste to put the gun down and bring the baby to Carmine, my finger got caught on the trigger and accidently sent a bullet ripping through the mattress. It scared me and forced me to face the fact that I was sprouting into wilted flowers of death. How could I ever think of taking Junior's life? Carmine was right. Who was I, and what was I going to do to change?

The walk to the bedroom I shared with Carmine was long and slow. I hugged and kissed Junior as he smiled at me. I instantly fell in love and bonded with him on a level I thought was impossible. Once I reached the bedroom door, I looked up at the ceiling and thanked God for showing up right on time. I could have lost so much that night but, in saving the baby, He saved me too. I reached for the knob, slowly pushed the door open, and almost fainted at the sight before me.

"Oh my God, Carmine, what are you doing?"

He sat in the chair dumbfounded. I walked to him too afraid to even touch him. We stared into each other's eyes and cried.

"I thought you killed him, Billie. I thought he was gone," Carmine wept.

I placed Junior in his arms and brought Carmine's head to my stomach. His tears wet my belly as I brushed my hands through his hair and kissed his head. When I first walked into the room, Carmine sat with his gun pointing at the door. A few seconds later, after realizing the baby was still alive, he turned the gun on himself. His eyes filled with disgrace, as if he was ashamed for allowing himself to lose faith in me.

"You were going to leave me, Carmine? How could you even think of doing that? Don't you know that I would die without you? Don't ever do that again, baby, please. I beg you."

I hadn't even given the thought of him pointing the gun at me much thought yet. Although that part would eventually seep into my reality and cause me to look at our relationship a bit differently, at that moment I just couldn't face life without him, and that thought prevailed.

As Carmine cried, he answered through his tears. "I wouldn't be able to live knowing that my love wasn't enough to stop you, Billie. Tonight, I sat in this room and thought of killing you. I thought of killing you, can you believe that? I couldn't bring myself to do it, so I was going to take your place. But when I saw the baby in your arms, I cursed myself for believing that you were evil enough to kill him, I'm so sorry, Billie. I am so sorry."

My heart was broken. Not because he thought of murdering me, but because I had pushed the only man I had ever truly loved, the only man who had ever deeply loved me, to this point. What would become of me? What would become of us if we didn't get off this path? For the first time since this journey began, I was truly afraid. An insignificant amount of anger toward Carmine did find its way to my heart the more I thought about him wanting to kill me over the baby. I tried to mask it as hurt, but something told me that this snowflake would snowball into something much more dangerous than hurt feelings. But that day, I would concentrate on the pain I caused him.

"I am the one who is sorry, Carmine. This all happened because of me. I am so sorry, my love. Forgive me."

That night, Carmine and I both faced the reality of what and who we had become. The scariest part was we would become comfortable with the inevitable.

Chapter 24

The Price of Brotherly Betrayal

Carmine and I had fallen asleep with baby Junior between us. It was a peaceful night and sleep came easy, as if our souls were exhausted and dying for a full night's rest. Carmine and I spent the evening coddling the baby and admiring him for everything he would repair in us. We'd raise him as our own and provide him with everything we were planning on giving Zen. The last thing we spoke about before dozing off was his new name. We had to come up with the perfect name.

When the alarm sounded, I looked at the clock and jumped up. The sound of shattering glass confirmed that there was an intruder.

"Carmine, wake up. Someone has broken in. Turn off the alarm before the police are called."

He followed my instructions. To some, not wanting the police around while your house was being broken into may have seemed weird, but the last thing we needed was to have the law sniffing around.

"Take the baby and hide him. Stay here and I'll go check it out," Carmine ordered.

"No, wait. I'll put him deep into the closet and I'll come with you. We're stronger together."

Carmine smiled as he watched me head for the closet. Once Junior was tucked away safely, Carmine picked up Zen's gun. Slowly and quietly, we made our way downstairs hoping to spot the intruder before he spotted us. We could hear his footsteps, but in the darkness we couldn't tell where they were coming from. Once on the lower floor, Carmine and I split up. I headed for the kitchen to grab my favorite weapon while he checked the living room and dining room areas.

I had just made it to the knives when someone yanked me backward by my shirt. Sharp hard blows plunged into my head and back as I screamed out for Carmine.

"I am going to kill you, bitch."

The voice was familiar, but I could not concentrate with the pain that was exploding through my body. I screamed for Carmine before receiving a blow to the face.

"I'm going to kill him too. You think that you could just murder my family and get away with it?"

The light flickered on as I was thrown to the ground. Dexter, Marley's brother, stood above me and landed a well-placed kick to the gut. I gasped for air as he kneeled down and began punching me in the face. Soon after, I would feel the blade of his knife sliding into my hand, as I tried to push him away from me.

"You killed them. You killed them all. Even Junior. You killed Junior," Dexter sang as his rage filled his fists with untamed power. If it weren't for Carmine running into the kitchen and firing a shot into his arm, God only knows what he would have done to me.

When Dexter grabbed his arm and screamed out in pain, Carmine walked up behind him and aimed the gun at his head.

"No. No, don't kill him. Not yet," I screeched as I held on to my face.

Carmine turned the gun around, cracked Dexter over the head with the butt, and knocked him out cold.

"Help me up, Carmine. We need to tie him to the chair."

I was dizzy from the blows to the face. Blood dripped from my mouth, nose, and hand, but I had to help Carmine pick the big man up. Once Carmine had him tied in place securely, he helped me clean up. He bandaged my hand, and got me an ice pack for my swelling face. On our way to the bathroom, we noticed the body of the one guard who watched over the house. Dexter had stabbed him in the neck and ended his life before getting to me. I knew that, from that moment on, we would be guarded just as well as the president. The Vegas and Bellissima didn't give their lack of security too much thought and look where it landed them: dead. I would never take this chance again. In the morning, I would hire the best of the best to guard our lives; but first, I had to deal with Dexter.

My body was aching with discomfort. I took a few pain pills hoping they would kick in soon. Dexter was still knocked out with his wrists, ankles, and chest tied to the chair he sat on. The pain was becoming unbearable so I asked Carmine to wake him up. With a sharp blow to the face, Dexter awoke to find me sitting directly in front of him. He took a few seconds to look around. Once Dexter realized where he was and what had happened, he spit at my feet. I looked at Carmine and he knew exactly what I wanted him to do. While he punched Dexter in the ribs, I spoke.

"You can choose to die peacefully, or you can go the hard way."

"Just . . . just turn . . . just turn me loose and I'll show you what I . . . what I can do, rotten bitch. You fucking whore. You . . . you should have stuck to pushing pussy, dirty slut. Bitch. I'm going . . . I'm going to kill you!" Dexter yelled, struggling to catch his breath.

I smiled at him through the pain. "Dexter, honey, I need you to step into the real world. No one is going to untie you. You are going to die, right there, in that chair, tonight."

After a few more insults were flung my way, I decided to stop playing with him. "So, you came all the way to L.A. to kill me because I murdered your brother?" I asked with amusement.

He now looked me dead in my eyes and told the truth. "You should have been expecting me, don't you think? You killed my brother, his wife, and the child. How could you? I thought you all settled that shit between you two at the meeting with Capello. Did it really have to go this far? You're an irrational bitch. To kill a baby, that is pure evil."

I could feel my heart rate picking up, which wouldn't be good news for Dexter. I tried to stay calm as I sent a rebuttal his way. "Your filthy, disgusting, child-molesting brother killed my baby. He sent that doctor here to have sex with a child, which caused her to feel so violated that she killed herself; yet, you ask me why? I killed them because they took my heart from me. I killed them because they are sick people who shouldn't walk this fucking earth. If you are sitting here asking me why that must mean that you are just like them. Are you?"

My chest bounced up and down with anticipation. Not that his answer would have changed anything, but I wanted to know who sat in front of me. He lowered his eyes and answered my question. "No, of course not, but that is the business we are in. That is the business that you are in too."

I fought to stand up while my blood started to boil. "No, that is the business I am trying to change. I will not sell underage children, and the people who will work for me will have a choice."

Dexter started to laugh. "Good luck on that, Billie. We'll see how long that lasts. You stand here as if what you will be doing will be any better than the system that is already in place. What, do you think those men and women who will be working for you are unscathed? What normal person do you know would pick prostitution as a career? You're fucking delusional."

His words hit me as if they were his fists. His comment was true, but I was unwilling to admit it, so I changed the subject. "So, to you, what your brother and his friend did is okay? If that's the case, me killing Junior should be fine with you, too."

Anger danced in his eyes once I mentioned the baby. Soon his eyes would be filled with sorrow. "No, that's not what I am saying; but, why the baby? Why did you have to kill the baby?"

His pain brought joy to my heart. I leaned into him, got close to his right ear, and whispered, "How do you know that I killed the little fucker?"

After speaking, I stood up and looked dead at him. I smiled as I watched tears leak from his eyes.

"When I got to my brother's place, the police were already there. They wouldn't let me go into the house, but my brother's next-door neighbor told me that everyone in the house was dead. When I asked for the baby, he said that he saw a blond woman and a black guy leave with Junior. At first, I felt a little relieved that Junior was still alive. But then, he told me that he saw the blonde drop something into the water, and that he thought it was the baby. How could you, Billie, how could you? My brother and his friend I understand, but why kill Alexa and the baby?"

I laughed inside. I could have told him that what I dropped in the water was the balled-up bloody shirt, but I got pleasure from his pain.

"So that's how you knew that it was Carmine and me? Those meddlesome neighbors, I tell you," I said as I shook my head. "You know what's interesting to me? You seem to be more heartbroken over Alexa and Junior than you are concerned over your own brother's death. What kind of brother are you?"

My words must have ripped him apart. Dexter started to cry as if his soul was being ripped from him. Carmine and I stood there, watching as snot and tears merged.

"How can a man care more for his nephew and sister-in-law than his own fucking brother?" Carmine asked, sounding just as surprised as me.

Dexter continued to cry while mumbling under his breath.

"What? What did you say?" I asked, but he did not answer. His inarticulate sounds seemed like gargle from his mouth, and that only irritated me. I looked around the room, and spotted the scissors that sat on the table. I rushed to pick them up, walked back over to Dexter and, with a hard, fast thrust of the hand, plunged them into his thigh.

"What were you just saying?" I asked angrily.

"My son. He was my fucking son."

I looked at Carmine. Carmine looked at me, and I started to laugh loudly. "Are you fucking kidding me? You were having an affair with your brother's wife? Goddamn, you are just as sleazy as Marley." This was turning into a damn soap opera. There wasn't a decent one in the bunch.

"No, it wasn't like that. I loved her first. My brother took her from me. I would have given her the world, but she chose him. What made it worse was that he treated her like shit most of the time. Cheated on her and disrespected her right in front of her face. I even think he was to blame for her having all of the miscarriages. She was always stressing over him and what he was doing. The more babies she lost, the worse his treatment toward her got. I tried to tell her to just leave him, and that I would take care of her, but she never did."

"So when does you having sex with Alexa and getting her pregnant come into play?" I asked as I hung off of every word. The most he could do was entertain me before I killed him.

"She came to me for comfort after she lost the last baby. It had been years since I touched her body. It . . . it just happened. Once she found out that she was pregnant, I wanted her to tell my brother about us, but she wouldn't. I didn't have the heart to do it because that would mean hurting her."

I sat down on the chair again and tried to process Dexter's drama.

"How were you able to just play the uncle role?" Carmine asked.

Dexter sobbed, but continued to speak. "It killed me every day for the past seven months, but it made her so happy. It took everything in me not to fall into a deep depression. In a way, I was proud that my seed was the only one who survived. In another way, I died a little every time I was around them. I tried to stay away, but eventually I would have to go over there. I just had to see him, hold him, and be with him. He was my son, and that woman should have been mine."

I looked at Dexter with pity spilling from my soul. "Your son is not dead. He's right here, in this house. Don't worry. No harm will come to him. Carmine and I will raise him as our own. He will have the best we can offer him. You can die knowing that he will be loved. We'll love him for you, Dexter. Do you hear me?"

Dexter wept like a baby. I thought of our son who slept peacefully upstairs in the safe hiding place and, instantly, his new name came to me. There was no need to prolong the inevitable. We would all be leaving our old lives behind and embarking on an unknown path. The only one who was certain of his future was Dexter. He knew death awaited him and it was now time for him to meet his Maker.

I looked at Carmine and nodded my head. I sort of felt bad for Dexter. He only came to do exactly what I did to his brother and the doctor. He came to avenge his son's death. That was when it became very clear to me that, no matter the person, good or bad, we all had a story. Too bad Dexter's ended with Carmine snapping his neck.

Chapter 25

The Price of Our Actions

I called Capello and told him in so many words that Dexter would no longer be around. I told him that he broke into our house and that I needed a clean-up crew to come over and take care of the mess. The minute those words left my mouth, Capello said that he would be over within the hour. Once I hung up with him, I asked Carmine to go upstairs and get the baby.

Since hearing his father's story, I just wanted to hug and kiss the little boy. He was alone in the world now, just like me. It was our duty to love him and give him everything Carmine and I lacked. Honestly, I couldn't say that I was completely in love with him yet, but at least I was able to look at him with love in my heart. Thinking about wanting to hurt that baby put the fear of God in me and reminded me of the place I never wanted to revisit again.

Carmine came back with the smiling baby and my heart melted. How could I have been so blind to this precious little boy and all the happiness he housed? Carmine sat beside me with Junior in his lap. As I played with the baby, Carmine smiled at me.

"You look happy, Billie. I am happy to see that," he said as he ran his fingers across the back of my neck.

"I know what we should call him," I answered with my own smile widening. "I think we should call him Zen. Zen Blue Pallazolo. That way, he will have the three entities of love surrounding him at all times."

I couldn't help but get a little choked up. While staring at the baby, I thought of what the name would mean. In calling him Zen, I was hoping that it would help me fully open my heart toward him. Blue would remind me of the old me and my mother. And with Carmine's last name, that made the baby a part of the man I loved most.

"I think it's perfect, Billie."

I took the baby from Carmine's arms and held him in mine. "Hi baby Zen. Can you say Mommy and Daddy?" I asked as I looked into his smiling face.

"Today is his birthday, Billie. I think that today should be known from here on out as his birthday. From what Dexter said, he's only seven months old. The baby will never know the difference."

Carmine put so much thought into what he was saying. He sounded like a little boy on Christmas Day, and that was priceless. This time, it was my turn to hit him with his infamous words.

"Whatever you want, baby. Whatever you want."

On August 1, 2005, at 5:03 a.m., Pacific Time, Zen Blue Pallazolo was born.

"What in the fuck is going on in this house? You can't just kill every damn person you come across, Billie."

I didn't mean to laugh, but Capello's statement came across a little funny.

"This is not funny. This is not how we run business over on this side of town. You are making some pretty important people very nervous. That's not a good look," Capello said very seriously.

"How can you blame me for killing the man who broke into our house? He came here to kill us. It was him or us. Who do you think we were going to choose?"

Carmine and I went over everything that happened starting at Marley's house. I told the truth, even about the darkest of events. We tried our best to make Capello understand that there was a reason behind everything we did.

"Look, Billie. It's not that I don't sympathize with everything that happened to Zen, but you can't go on like this. You have managed to kill off two partners in the matter of a week. Just like you have people to answer to, so do I."

I looked at Capello with a scrunched-up face. "Who do you answer to? I thought you were the boss."

Capello laughed at my ignorance. "See, this is why I need you to calm down and continue to learn. My father and uncle sit at the very top with another partner. They are old school and get spooked once blood starts to spill, unless it's absolutely necessary. They don't want any trouble, and when people begin to disappear, the cops will come snooping around. I was able to calm them down, but I don't know how many more times I'll be able to save your ass. I like you and Carmine and I think that the two of you will bring something new to the Pricey Pussy business, but you have to chill out."

It was a great feeling to hear that Capello liked us. It was like making our father proud.

"I thought you told us that all they do is sit back and collect money," I said, thinking back to an earlier conversation.

"What do you think real bosses do? They don't get their hands dirty. They delegate and stack their money," Capello answered.

"I'm sorry, but I had to do Marley and the doctor. They are the ones who hurt our little girl. As far as Dexter, he came and tried to hurt us. It was do or die."

Capello smiled and asked to hold the baby. "Is this Marley's kid?" he asked as he bounced Zen on his knee.

"No, this is our son. His name is Zen. We'll need a birth certificate for him," Carmine spoke up.

Capello looked from Carmine to me, and back to Carmine again. "Okay, I'll have the doctor come back out and treat this like a home birth."

"There are a few other things that need to be taken care of," I added. I went on to tell Capello about the security issue and how I just didn't feel safe with the baby in the house. I wanted seven armed men around the clock and guard dogs. I also wanted two men for our personal protection. They would make sure that Carmine, the baby, and I were safe at all times, no matter the chaos around us. If my plans went off without a hitch, Carmine and I would be taking the Pricey Pussy Empire by storm. We were sure to piss a few people off and make a hell of a lot of enemies in the near future.

"Is that it?" Capello asked before informing us that he had a plane to catch.

"We still have the issue of the neighbor who saw Carmine and me leaving Marley's house. We have to take care of that."

Capello sat back in his chair and thought about things. "Yeah, I suppose you're right, but this is the last one, Billie. No one else gets killed unless you clear it with me first, understood?"

I nodded my head yes.

"So, which neighbor was it?" Capello asked.

"Dexter never said which one," I answered.

"So, what do we do?" Capello asked as he looked at us.

His question gave me a sense of heightened power. My boss was asking me what should be done, and I loved how that made me feel.

"Kill them both. We shouldn't take a chance and end up letting the wrong one live."

Capello looked at me as if I were insane.

"Would you rather this neighbor give up information that would lead the police to us? If not, it must be done."

I knew that Capello was dead set against this but, somewhere in his eyes, I saw the truth. He realized that we really didn't have a choice.

"Billie, I'm not sure about this. I mean, you're talking about killing a man who may not have anything to do with this. We—"

"No, not just the man. You have to kill everyone in that house. You don't know what he's said to his wife. I'm sorry, but they all have to go."

"What if they have children?" Carmine asked.

I looked at him and made a deal. "Baby, I know that you don't want to harm children, so I want you to set an age limit. From this day on, no one under that age will die by our hands."

Carmine stood thinking and finally came up with an answer. "Thirteen. No one under thirteen should get killed."

I looked at Capello as if things were now settled. "Can you set everything up? Carmine has to get back to Florida to do the job."

"I have to run this over with my father and uncle. I am headed to Florida now so I'll make a call to my father. Carmine can come with me tonight. I'll call and have a few men stay with you until the guards get here."

With that, Carmine and I headed upstairs to pack him an overnight bag.

***

I walked Carmine to the door with baby Zen in my arms. Capello walked ahead to the car to give us a few minutes alone.

"Hurry back to us," I offered. I leaned into the man I loved and kissed his lips. We had been through so much. We went from slavery to freedom, from death to life, and from strangers to lovers. We stood in our union, unbreakable and solid, in that moment. Even when I was drowning in darkness, he and his love for me were the light that guided me through. I loved Carmine, and I couldn't wait until I loved little Zen, too.

"I love you, Billie Blue Blondie. And when I come back, I am going to marry you."

I couldn't believe what I heard. *Did he just say he wants to marry me?* I asked him to repeat himself just to make sure my ears weren't deceiving me.

"You heard me, beautiful. When I get back, I am going to make you my wife. Let's face it. We are the only ones who could put up with the other. You complete me, and I complete you. There's no way around it, Mrs. Pallazolo."

My heart raced as I leaned in and kissed Carmine again. For the first time since the last time I slept in my mother's arms, I felt complete.

"Get back to me as quickly as you can. I love you, Carmine."

"I love you too," he answered as he pulled away from me and walked to the waiting car.

The vehicle started to pull off but came to an abrupt stop. The driver stepped out and opened the car door. Capello stepped out of the car and walked back over to me.

"What's wrong?" I questioned.

"The plans have changed a bit. I just got a call and you have to come with me," Capello answered, gripping my arm firmly.

"Let go of me, Capello. You're going to make me drop the baby!" I yelled.

For the first time since meeting him, I was frightened by what I saw in his eyes.

"My father called and he wants to see you."

My heart dropped as Capello's warning played over in my mind, but I wouldn't let him smell my fear. Instead, I offered an excuse. "I can't leave the baby."

Capello yanked baby Zen from my arms and called out for one of his guards. "Take the baby to one of the girls and tell her to guard him with her life. Stay here and watch over them and make sure nothing goes wrong."

When I started to scream, I saw the car door fly open behind Capello's frame. Carmine fought to get out but two men held him in the car.

"Don't be difficult, Billie. I told you this may happen. You have killed two partners, and you went too far."

"But . . . but . . ." I fought to stay in the house but Capello was dragging me out. Once I was out of the front door, another guard came over and helped him get me inside of the car.

"What in the fuck is going on?" Carmine yelled to Capello.

The minute I got in the vehicle, I latched on to Carmine, who was still being held down by the men. It was crowded in the back seat and I felt as if I couldn't breathe. After asking one of the men to exit the car, there were only four of us left in the back. Capello was at one end, us in the middle, and a guard by the other door.

"That phone call that I got, it was my father. I have to take you two in," Capello said, answering Carmine.

"Don't let him do this, Carmine. He made me leave Zen with one of the girls."

I was pleading with Carmine with more than just my voice. In my eyes, he saw everything that he needed to see. He began fighting the one man who was holding him back. He put up a good struggle but, with one swift motion, the man who had exited the car raised his gun and slammed the butt of it into the back of

Carmine's head. When I saw his body go limp, and blood leak on his shirt, I screamed and tried to wake him up.

"Don't even bother, Billie. He'll be out for most of the ride," Capello said as the car pulled off.

I looked at the man who I should have known was dangerous. He was the son of the ultimate boss, for crying out loud. He was also a major player in the seedy underground world that had ruined me. I should have never underestimated him, or the advice he gave.

"Why are you doing this?" was all that I managed to get out.

Capello took a deep breath and, while doing so, looked me in the eyes. This time, I recognized the man I was staring at. The soft side of him appeared before me again. "I tried to tell you that this would happen, Billie. You just wouldn't listen. I can't lie and say that I know exactly what will happen once we arrive at my family's compound, but I'll ask that the both of you walk out alive."

I wanted to cry out of fear, but fright was a fleeting emotion. The more we drove, the angrier I became, and rage would show itself at the wrong time once again.

Chapter 26

The Price of Playing in Traffic

It took us only forty-five minutes to reach one of the Capello estates. The compound was beautiful, with a green luscious lawn and a gorgeous house sitting at the top of the hill; but, admiring what they had gained from the sweat, tears, and souls of stolen boys and girls wasn't on my agenda. Instead, my heart raced and my head spun at the thought of what could possibly happen to me and the man I loved.

Carmine was awakened with smelling salts. Coming out of his slumber, he was confused and in pain. "Where are we?" he asked, holding the back of his head.

After I explained everything to Carmine, it all seemed to come rushing back to him. As we exited the car, he spoke truthful words to Capello. "I'll die before I let anything happen to Billie. You do know that, right?"

Capello didn't answer with words. He nodded his head while the guards told us to follow them.

The inside of the home felt cold and looked as if it hadn't been decorated since the eighties. It was beautiful and the furnishings and decorations looked expensive, but I could tell that the Capellos were stuck in a different decade.

"You two, wait here with my men. One of them will get you something for your head, Carmine. I'll go in the study and speak to them first," Capello said, pointing at the two seats outside of a heavy wooden door. The hallway we stood in was dimly lit by little lights with tiny shades, which hung on the walls surrounding us. While we sat down, I watched as Capello straightened his suit and tie before entering the study.

"Are you okay, baby?" I asked Carmine while he tried to wipe away the blood from the back of his head and neck with the towel that was given to him.

"I'll be fine. I can't worry about my head right now. We have to stay alert," he answered in a serious tone.

The men who watched over us laughed. I went to speak but Carmine's hand on my knee stopped me. "Pay them no mind, Billie. Let them laugh. They are only trying to distract us."

I followed his instructions and stayed quiet. We would wait almost thirty minutes to enter the study. I tried my best to hear what was being said in there but the heavy doors only allowed me to hear muffles.

Once Capello came back into the hallway, he was followed by three huge men who wore firearms on their hips. One grabbed me, and the other two gripped Carmine by each of his arms.

"Is that necessary?" Capello asked.

The men said that they were following orders, and then dragged us into the study. The two older men, who I presumed were the uncle and father, sat at desks opposite from each other. We were thrown to the ground in the middle of both of them. I tried to stand up but received a sharp kick to the back of my left calf, causing me to fall to my knees again. I cried out in pain. Carmine tried to come to my aid but received the same treatment.

"Just stay down, Billie," Capello demanded.

I was seething with anger. The thought of having to stay down on my knees in front of the two men who destroyed my life was something I just couldn't swallow. My pride was at war with my brain. I knew that my best and safest bet would be to stay quiet and listen, but I sat on my knees wondering how long my brain would have the upper hand.

"She's definitely a fighter," a dense yet feminine voice echoed.

I hadn't noticed anyone else in the room besides the two men. When I turned to the right, I saw a woman, smoking a long, skinny cigarette. Her beauty was striking, but behind the allure of her gorgeous face were eyes that looked deadly. She was sprawled out on a lounge chair, dressed in a long white gown as if she was in the 1920s. Diamonds hung from her neck, ears, fingers, and wrists. Her hair was jet-black, and stood out against her pale white skin.

"Looks like this fighter has picked the wrong opponent," one of the gray-haired men spoke.

I glared at him, unwilling to lower my eyes. He laughed at me, letting me know that I did not intimidate him. "Little girl, I am not Bobby. Your tantrums will not move me. You wanted to play with the boys; now you'll have to handle this like a fucking man."

The one who spoke was the thinnest of the men. I watched him leave his seat and walk around the desk. He leaned on the edge of it before me and spoke again. "I am Sammy, Bobby's uncle. I have been waiting to lay eyes on the little girl who is causing so much havoc. You are as beautiful as my nephew said you were, and your attitude is just as ugly."

I looked up at the tall, lean man and scrunched my face in disgust. There were so many things I could have said to him but I felt two words would be enough. "Fuck you," I snarled before spitting at his feet.

"Stand her up!" the woman called out.

I watched as she put her cigarette out. She frowned at me, her eyes throwing daggers of anger in my direction. I tried to pull away from the man who held my arms behind my back but his grip was strong. She walked over to me slowly, readjusting the rings on her fingers. Once she reached me, I smiled at the woman who looked to be no younger than fifty years old.

"What in the fuck are you going to do to me, you old bitch?" I huffed.

The older woman lifted both her hands and balled them in to fists. Her diamonds hit the lights above us and seemed to light the way for the punches that landed on my face. She was vicious and fast. Blow after blow, each one seemed even harder than the last. I could hear Carmine cursing but he was unable to move from the spot the two men held him in.

"You disrespectful little bitch. You spit at my husband's feet?" she asked while pounding on my face. "I will fucking murder you, you whore of a slave. Do you know who we are? Huh, do you?"

Blow after blow, I could feel her rings tearing into my face. I tried my best to move my face away but with my hands behind my back, I couldn't shield it from her fists.

"Esperanza, that is enough, darling," Sammy called out to his wife.

Like a robot, she stopped, slipped the rings off her bloody hands, set them on the desk, and went back to her seat. She wiped her blood-stained fingers on her white gown and then lit another cigarette. The fat man who was still sitting at his desk got up, and joined his brother.

"Bobby, this is who you bring into our organization? This girl has no self-control. She is a ticking bomb."

"Father, she may be wild, but I believe that I made the right decision. I agree that she needs training and time to grow, but she's the right one for the job." Capello's voice had a tremor in it, and that was something I had never heard before.

"I am finding it hard to see what it is that you see in her. She's just a mutt. She likes to bark and, if you let her, she'll bite."

With blood running down my face, and pain ripping through my system, I still managed to be defiant. "You motherfucker, let me go and I'll show you how hard I bite! Fucking monsters, all of you. You did this to me, each and every one of you. This is who you created!" I screamed.

"Billie, shut the hell up," Capello pleaded.

While all the attention was on me, Carmine had managed to free himself from the two men. He ran toward me, landed a few blows to the face of the man who held my hands behind my back, and Carmine was able to grab his gun. I clung to him as he swung his arm around and pointed the gun at Sammy. While doing so, every gun in the room pointed at us.

"If anyone touches her again, I will kill you."

The air in the room was thick with anxiety and scorching with anticipation.

"Look around, son. You are surrounded. Even my sister-in-law has a gun pointing at you. Put the weapon down and we can talk this through," Capello's father said with certainty.

When we looked over to the lounge chair, sure enough, Esperanza was pointing a gun at us. Her eyes seemed to zero in on Carmine's trigger finger.

"Sir, I don't want to be rude but you're full of shit. Were you just planning on talking to us while that bitch beat on Billie?" Carmine asked with a steady hand.

"Call me Domenico. I am a man of my word. If you put the gun down, I can promise you two things. One: the both of you will pay for pointing that gun in my brother's face and for being so disrespectful. Two: you will not die in this house. I promise you that much. Nor will you die by our hands," Capello's father promised.

"It's a trick, Carmine. Don't put it down," I whispered to him.

Carmine seemed confused when it came to putting the gun down. He stared at the man and seemed like he was trying to read his thoughts. "Sir, how do I know I can trust you? We are nothing to you. We are just slaves who outsmarted our captors. Killing us would be like ordering a pizza to you," Carmine reasoned.

"Look, we don't know each other but I have built this life based on my word. I am telling you that if you put down the gun, we will not kill you, or Billie. After what you two have shown us tonight, I would love to . . . have a talk. If not, my men will fill your body with holes, understand?" the big man asked.

It took a few minutes for Carmine to make up his mind. I was shaking my head no, while Capello tried to reason with us. "Do as my father says, Carmine. He does not lie. Just put it down, please! Billie, tell him to put the gun down."

I could not in good faith instruct Carmine to lower the gun. My face was on fire and if that was any proof of what those people were capable of, there was no way in hell I was willing to drop the gun.

"Listen to him," the old woman sang.

"Do I have your word?" Carmine asked Domenico.

"You have my word," he answered.

Slowly, Carmine's arm lowered. Capello came to him and took the gun out of his hand. The minute the weapon was secured, punches rained down on Carmine unmercifully. I was once again being held back by two men, while others entered the room to join in on the beat down Carmine was receiving. I screamed for him, I begged them to stop, and I even called out for Capello. But nothing would be done to help him.

"You fucking liar! Please, stop. Oh my God, I am going to fucking kill you all," I continued to holler.

"Take her to the basement now!" Sammy yelled.

The two men who held on to me started to drag me out of the room. I kicked, I screamed, I used my legs to knock over anything that was near, but I couldn't stop them.

"Carmine, Carmine! Don't you die on me! I know you'll get us out of this! Do you hear me, Carmine? Please, let me go, let me go!"

I was hauled out of the study while fighting to get loose, but also while pleading for Carmine to rescue us. Soon after, I would find myself in a dark basement, chained to a wall, realizing that I was right back to the hell I had escaped. The cellar I was in may have been in a different house, but there I was, chained beneath another home, not knowing if I would live to see the next day.

Chapter 27

Carmine

The Price of Devotion

I didn't think that I would survive the beating, but that didn't matter to me. My life was not my worry. My mind was on Billie. If I didn't make it, what would happen to her? I heard her cries while they pulled her out the room. It crushed me to hear her call for help, while I was unable to do anything about it.

"Okay, boys, sit him in the chair," I heard Sammy call out.

I could hardly stand up. The beating that felt like hours only lasted two minutes or so. Once seated in the chair, two men stood on both sides of me. Sammy and his brother took their seats behind their desks and just stared at me. I was unable to talk and I waited for one of them to break the silence. Capello spoke up before the two powerful men. Taking a seat beside me, he tried to make me understand why Billie and I were in the position we were in.

"I tried to warn her, Carmine, but she just wouldn't listen. You can't kill partners and think that nothing will happen," Capello said with his eyes to the ground.

"My son is softhearted. This is why you are here right now. Do you think that if we wanted you dead, you would ever make it to our residence? What were you and your girlfriend thinking pointing a gun at my head? People have died for much less," Sammy questioned.

Through the pain, I thought of their words. It was hard to concentrate with my body aching and my mind on Billie. "If . . . if you are going to kill us, just do it," was all I said.

The room was silent before Domenico's laughter came crashing down. "I told you that you had my word that we would not kill you or Billie. Your mistrust will be the end of you. I know that we are in a fucked-up business but, contrary to what some may think, there is honor among thieves. If you live long enough, you will learn this for yourself," the big man added.

"If you lived the life we've lived, you would understand why Billie reacted the way she did.

To be thrown down to our knees when we have only started to stand on our feet is an insult. We are victims of your so-called business. Of course there would be resentment," I spat between deeply inhaled breaths.

The room was silent again. I observed the woman who sat with the bloody white dress and I watched her smoke.

"My nephew has told me your story. Now I want to hear it from you," Sammy requested.

For the next thirty minutes or so, I struggled through the story of my journey with Billie. I told the truth about everything, from what happened in my aunt's house, to the buyers' circle. I even told them about Bellissima, Zen, what happened with the partners, and baby Zen. During my storytelling, the woman who chain-smoked and seemed uninterested while I spoke started to cry as I talked about Zen. I went into deep detail about losing her, how it made me feel, and how I felt a part of me had died with her. Esperanza's wails were deep-rooted, and I could tell that I struck a very sensitive portion of her soul. I continued to speak while her cries played as the background melody. I wasn't trying to win sympathy votes. I was just telling them the truth.

Suddenly, while I was in the middle of a sentence, the shrieking beauty got up and walked to her husband. With tears in her eyes, she told her husband that she was leaving to deal with Billie. I tried to stand to my feet but the pain stopped me.

"No, please, don't hurt her. I'll do whatever you want," I pleaded.

"She has to pay. She has to pay for disrespecting my husband," Esperanza said. She no longer seemed like the weak and hurt woman who had cried at my tale.

"Do whatever you want to me. I can handle it. Let me pay for what we both have done," I begged.

"You really mean that, don't you?" Domenico asked curiously.

"One hundred percent," I answered before continuing. "When I told Billie I would die for her, that's exactly what I mean."

"You certainly are devoted to this girl. What is it about her that has you willing to put yourself on the line?" Sammy asked.

I looked at the tall, thin man while thinking. His white hair was slicked back and not one hair was out of place. He stared back at me, outwardly fishing for the truth.

"Because, she is to me what the woman who stands by your side is to you. I see how you look at her; and, if you were in my place, you would do the same," I said, offering my reality.

For a while, no one spoke. I awaited my fate calmly, and without hesitation.

"I admire your dedication to Billie. And if you are sure that this is what you want, this is what you will get," Domenico answered.

I looked him dead in the eyes and would not waver on my decision. I didn't even have to answer; he saw my response in the vessel to my soul.

"Have a talk with Billie, Esperanza, but don't harm her," Sammy told his wife.

She exited the room, closing the door behind her. I held on to my ribs trying to pace my breath. "Can we get on with it? Capello and I have a flight to catch. I'm sure you know about the situation with the neighbor," I requested.

Strangely, Sammy smiled before speaking to me. "I like you, Carmine. Even at your age, you are a man. I'm sorry to do this, but it's the price you have to pay for your devotion to Billie." Turning to his guards, he told them what to do. "Go ahead, boys, take care of him. Don't break his arms or legs. He has a job to do once he leaves here."

The blows that crashed against my body that night caused inexplicable pain. I counted five men before falling out of the chair and hitting the floor. I was pummeled until I balled up and just yelled from the agony they caused. In any other circumstance, I would have fought back but, like Sammy said, I had to pay the tab Billie and I ran up. The beating lasted about ten minutes. I knew this because I stared at the clock on the wall through puffy eyes. When it was over, Sammy stood by my head and spoke.

"Let me tell you something about love, Carmine. With a girl like Billie holding the keys to your heart, one day she's going to force you to open the wrong damn door. What I saw in her pretty blue eyes is rare. She is a monster, Carmine, do you hear me? I know you think that because of that life you took on the boat it makes you a heartless creature like she is, but you're not. You still have a soul to save, Carmine, while hers no longer exists. I know my words seem harsh, and they should. Just know that I have dealt with a lot of evil in my line of work. Billie may have not started that way, but because of what she has been through, evil dwells within her now. Give me your hand, son, let me help you up," Sammy said with an outstretched arms.

It was hard, but I managed to stand to my feet. Blood streamed from my nose, mouth, and lips. My ribs felt like they were cracked, but I fought through the pain.

"I want you to come and see me every month. Bobby will be stepping back and I want you to deal directly with me. I don't normally do this, but you're young, and you need guidance. Also, no more killings unless we okay them first. This is a fucking business, and we run this shit, not you. You two work for us, and we don't kill anyone unless we have no choice. This is your final warning. Next time, I will make sure the both of you are killed. When you come and see me, never bring Billie with you unless I tell you to, understand?"

I looked Sammy in the eyes and told him that I understood every word.

Chapter 28

The Price of It All

The basement was cold and dark. Looking around, I felt as if there wasn't enough oxygen down there. Never did I think that I would end up chained in a basement again. It brought back too many memories of the Vega home. I would have rather they kill me than chain me up like a slave once more.

When I heard the door open at the top of the stairs, I was relieved. If it was death that awaited me, I wanted it to happen fast. I'd rather anything but another lifetime in a cellar. I heard the sound of her shoes first. When she appeared, her hair was pulled back and her eyes were a devil's red. She dragged a metal chair that sat against one of the walls behind her, and set it directly in front of me. I could hardly look in to her eyes. They were dark and seemed dead.

"Hello again, Billie. I want to have a little chat with you," she said while I looked away from her. "Look at me when I talk to you, little girl."

I tried to do as she asked, but the sorrow in her eyes caused me to look away the minute we made eye contact. She laughed. It was hearty and deep-rooted.

"Do you know the reason you have a hard time looking at me? Do you, Billie? Well, let me tell you why. It is because you see yourself in me. I was once the girl you are now, and I am what you will become," Esperanza explained.

I stole glances at her before letting her know how I felt. "You're so full of shit. We are nothing alike. I'm so sick of you people thinking that I have something in common with you. You don't even know me," I spat.

She lit her cigarette before filling me in on the details I didn't know about her. "I was you, Billie, and I still am. Maybe you're even a little stronger than me. See, you fought for your freedom, even killed for it. Mine was handed to me by that man you know as my husband. He rescued me, married me, and made me his equal," Esperanza proudly boasted.

"What in the fuck is wrong with these men? Do they get off by so-called rescuing sex slaves?" I asked in disgust.

"Maybe. I really don't know what it is. Maybe they like playing the hero, as Carmine loves playing for you. Maybe they think we'll forever be indebted to them so, therefore, we'll always love them. I don't know what it is, to tell you the truth, but I am thankful for Sammy," she answered.

I didn't know what to say. It was starting to dawn on me how fucked up the underworld of human trafficking was. Even as a victim herself, Esperanza made herself believe that her husband was her hero, even as he continued to victimize other men, women, and children.

"I know that look in your eyes, and I know what it means. But the longer you spend in the business, the more you will understand. And you and I are connected for more than one reason, Billie. Carmine told us your stories, and by the time he got to Zen, I could hardly breathe. I know what it's like to have buried a child. Sammy and I lost our only son."

When she said this, finally, I stared into her eyes. What I found in them would stay with me for the rest of my life. In them, I saw my pain. I didn't speak, and neither did she for a few minutes. But soon, she would continue.

"Upstairs, when you disrespected my husband, forcing me to strike you, I need you to understand why I reacted the way I did. The minute you walked into the study, a chill came over me. I was gazing at the young girl I used to be, and it angered me. Outside of you being ill-mannered and wild, I also came face to face with all of the pain I have tried to forget. I don't know if you know this now, Billie, but you are ruined. If you are still looking for the girl you used to be, I need you to know that she is gone. You won't find her in that new baby you have at home, you won't find her in Carmine, and you will never find her in yourself. Don't look to others while searching for who you are. Look in the mirror and accept who you have become. Are you listening to me, Billie? I need you to listen closely."

"Yes, I am listening," I answered.

"I need you to take control of yourself because, right now, you are like a dog, foaming at the mouth. You come off as wanting to tear apart anyone who you think deserves it, but haven't you had enough? Look at your bandaged hand. You came in already beaten and hurt. Don't get me wrong. In a way, that is good. You are a woman entering one of the most underhanded businesses known to man. Men won't respect you, and they'll think that because you are a woman, they can shit on you. That is when you'll have to show them your fangs and let them know that you are never afraid to bite. But you will also have to know how to control your bark. Never disrespect the people above you or you'll end up dead; and if you ever even raise your voice at my husband or his brother again, I'll be the one to slit your throat."

Nothing in her voice told me that she wasn't serious. The look in her eyes told me that, just like me, she was lifeless inside and wouldn't think twice of taking my life. While in my own thoughts, I had failed to notice her standing up. The men who had entered the basement with her stood close behind her, just in case. With her right hand, Esperanza squeezed each side of my mouth until it hurt.

"Be smart, Billie. You have already lost so much. Don't make me have to take the life that resembles my own. I want you to thrive, Billie, but I will also fucking kill you if I have to."

With that, she slapped me a few times, I'm guessing to enforce her words. Her hand was heavy, and caused my face to sting and my lips to start bleeding all over again.

"Unchain her, and bring her upstairs," she barked at her men. Esperanza climbed the stairs calmly as if she hadn't just ended our little chat with several slaps to my face. Esperanza's men did as they were told. I didn't know how to feel about the people who were now our bosses. That night would change how I handled things, not out of fear, but out of the respect they demanded. I knew that things had to change, and with Capello leaving to go full throttle with the porn thing, I would really have to watch my temper. Capello wasn't lying when he said that he was the nice one. Once upstairs, Carmine's was the first face I saw. I screamed his name and ran to him. He could hardly stand on his own but, still, he reached out and held me.

"Oh my God, Carmine. What did they do to you? Are you okay?" I asked, already knowing that he wasn't. His face was swollen, his shirt was bloody, and he looked like he wanted to pass out.

"I'm fine, Billie Blue. Don't you worry about me," Carmine said, forcing a smile.

"Say your good-byes. Carmine has to go with Capello to take care of that problem," Sammy said impatiently.

"Are you kidding me? He can't take care of that looking like this. You almost beat him to death. He can't—"

"Billie, I am fine. Do as he says, and I'll be home as soon as I'm done."

Carmine's voice was forceful and stern. I could tell by the look in his face that he wanted me to shut up. I was still learning to stay in my place, and I would also have to learn that Carmine was a man. The time of us being children, a boy and a girl, was now over. We now had to be woman and man.

When I looked to Sammy and his wife, he looked at Carmine proudly, realizing that Carmine was a fast learner. I looked back at my man, and I knew that I would have to get used to him also stepping into his own and accept the fact that, just like me, he was his own warrior. So instead of running my mouth, I kissed his swollen lips.

"I'll be waiting for you, baby. Come home soon," I said, pulling away from him.

"Don't worry, Billie. He'll make it back to you safely. I have faith in him. Once he's home, I'll send over a guy to do your tattoos. This is the real deal, kids. There's no going back now," Sammy added, holding out his arm.

"I don't see anything," I answered.

Sammy came close to me, pulled his keys from his pocket, and turned on a little black light that hung from the keychain. He shined the light on his forearm and there it was. It was a tattoo of a stick figure playing in traffic. Carmine stared at his arm, and then one by one, Capello, his father, and Esperanza all held out their arms. Sammy shined the light on all of their arms and one after the other, allowed us to see their matching tattoos. I now knew what the guard saw on Capello's arm at the buyers' circle.

After, I was taken to the waiting car with two guards, and was driven back home.

Once I got in the house, I rushed to the bathroom to clean and bandage my face before seeing baby Zen. Parts of my face was swollen and cut, but nothing Esperanza had done would leave a scar. After I was done, I went downstairs and waited for the girl who had been watching over Zen to bring him to me. He smiled the minute he saw me. I thought that maybe the bandages on my face would scare him, but he wasn't bothered by them at all.

I went to the kitchen and fixed the baby a bottle and grabbed a bag of frozen peas for my face. After, I headed upstairs to lie with Zen and watch television. Passing Bellissima's old room, something made me stop. I looked in the room without stepping inside. The gloom radiating from her old chambers gave me chills. As I stood there, Zen started to cry. He cried as if something bit him and he was in horrible pain. I realized that evil dwelled in that room and it gave me chills. I hurried and pulled the door shut and vowed not to ever go in there again. I would keep that promise until I broke it.

I spent all of my time with baby Zen while Carmine was gone. His smile pulled me in and was forcing me to love him. Every time I looked at him, I saw God, and that gave me a little faith. Now all I needed was for Carmine to get back home so we could put an end to what was, and start on what was always meant to be. My journey to America, living a nightmare, Carmine's birth and circumstances with his family, losing Zen, and finding her again in baby Zen: it was all destined to be. I believed in fate now more than ever.

When my phone rang the next morning and Carmine told me the job was done, I only had a few words to offer. "Come on home, baby. We're waiting for you." Finally, Carmine and I had a family to call our own again. This time, nothing but death would tear us apart.

The next few months were total bliss. Our business thrived, the money started to come in, we were making the bosses happy, and we had managed to stay in the light and become a happy family. If only someone told us that the best of times were behind us. The flesh market is one of the dirtiest games, but we would soon become expert players. But then again, I guess Capello did his best to warn us. We just never listened.

Slowly, we learned that once you are at the top, the people below become tired of raising their heads to look at you. Soon, their necks will start to hurt and they'll do anything to pull you down to their level so they can take your place. Their only trouble was, once we were down on flat ground, we would kill them and use their bodies as stepstools to regain our seats on our thrones as the King and Queen of the Pricey Pussy Empire. The next ten years would be some of the most chaotic years of our lives but, as always, we survived and remained free. As the saying goes, "Freedom is what you do with what's been done to you." As for Carmine and me, we used our freedom to do what no other partner had ever done before. We used it to pave our own path.

Epilogue

The Price of Enlightenment

"So you see, Bobbi, I am more than just a pretty face. So tell me. What is the difference between my spot in hell and where you stand? We all burn just the same. Our scars may be different, being that you wear yours on the outside; but when they are on the inside, they are harder to get to. The pain I feel from all that I have been through will never go away, just as yours lingers and stays. We are all damaged, all three of us. No one at this table is clear from destruction. We all hurt people because we are hurt people. You do it in the form of drugs, and I do it in the form of selling pussy and dick."

Bobbi sat silently for a while. Throughout our life story, I watched her closely for signs of emotion. At times, she showed some, but at other parts of the story, she showed none. I was curious as to why some parts of our lives affected her so deeply, while at other parts she seemed to want to run and hide. I wondered what made her so uncomfortable with our truth.

"Honestly, I am rather shocked. I would have never guessed that all of this happened to you two. Tell me, are you all going through life with a mask on or were you able to overcome it all?" Bobbi asked.

I looked at her dead on and answered truthfully. "I wear mine sometimes. It's safer that way. How about you, Carmine?" I asked as I turned to him.

"I think that we will always have to wear a mask to a certain degree. The world would not be able to handle us if we showed what it has done to us. Think of a murderer who is not a sociopath. If he were to ever face his victim's family, the weight of his sin would be too heavy. That is what we have become: the world's victims. So we wear our masks to hide from what we really are."

Stillness fell upon the room. We all seemed to be letting the words Carmine spoke soak in.

"So what happened when you left with Capello? How was it, taking care of the neighbors?" Bobbi asked Carmine.

"The trip went smoothly. After, he took me to his father's house for a few hours, per his uncle's request. We spoke about the business and about Billie. Once business was out of the way, Sammy and I played chess and spoke about some personal things."

"Like what?" I asked. Carmine and I had never spoken about his trip outside of me asking if everything was taken care of.

"We spoke mostly about you and the kind of woman you are. He told me about his wife, why he feels she is just like you, and what happened with their son. He asked me if I could love you 'til death. I told him yes; my own. I said that I would much rather die than see any harm come your way. He said he believed me after the beat down I took for you."

I looked at Carmine with love dripping from my eyes. "What did he say to that?" I asked.

"He told me that the love we have, it's the most dangerous kind of love. He said that he completely understood it though, because that was the kind of love he and his wife share."

I couldn't help but reach out and grab his hand. Yes, our love was dangerous, but everything that is worthwhile is never 100 percent safe.

"I still see him once a month. We have grown close since then. He is like the father I never had. We handle business and, after, we talk about life," Carmine added with a grin.

"So what happened with the neighbors?" Bobbi asked.

"I killed them all. Thank God neither had kids," Carmine answered nonchalantly.

"Now what, Bobbi? You know everything about us. Where does that leave . . . this?" I asked, wanting to feel her out.

"That's some real messed-up stuff you've been through. I could never imagine being in your shoes, but we all have a story to tell. You may see my scars, but believe me when I tell you that I have plenty that's hidden. Just as you and Carmine were forced into a life you didn't want, well, that's what my face represents. Love turned me into this weird-looking monster. And, just like you two, I was held captive and tricked into my situation. I only have a few more questions before I give you the chance to learn who I really am. What made you continue on this path? You seem so damaged by what has been done to you. How could you become a madam, and have Carmine carry out your dirty deeds?"

I thought about her questions for a short while before the answer dawned on me. "There is a quote by Voltaire that goes, 'It is difficult to free fools from the chains they revere.' It just took us a long while to realize that we are those fools."

Seemingly satisfied with my answer, she looked away from us. Suddenly, her soul appeared the moment she began to unravel and reveal herself. This was the story that would eventually lead her to this very point in her life. It was then that we really had the chance to look at the scars she kept hidden. We also noticed that these marks ran much deeper than the ones left behind for the rest of the world to see.

{A Note from the Author}

When Billie and Carmine came to me engulfed in darkness, I didn't know where these two characters would lead me. So I sat back, listened, and wrote their story as it came to me. Once it hit me that I was penning a story on sex slaves and human trafficking, I stopped and thought about things. I didn't know how to continue writing the story without going to the most sadistic and depraved places within my own mind. I would have to dig deep and leave sanity behind in order to form a connection with Billie and Carmine. That was the only way to stay true to the characters and keep the story authentic.

Some may never understand the lives of these teens or the choices they've made so far. Some will never comprehend the mind of the wounded, and I have to come to terms with that. As I did research in preparation for *Pricey*, my head hurt and my heart filled with gloom. At the time of my research, it was reported that there were

35.8 million slaves in the world, and that half of the people being trafficked across international waters were children under the age of 18. That was completely shocking to me. The statistics on human trafficking are heart wrenching, and as I wrote *Pricey*, I found myself arguing with the characters. But I also knew that I had to take everything that I had learned and force the world to face the hard truths through this story. While some may wonder how children could do the things Billie and Carmine have done, I must remind them that after living through certain things, these characters are no longer children. Their age may tell you one thing about them, but the life they have lived has stripped them of all innocence.

At times, I could not come to terms with the choices Billie and Carmine made. Although I wanted to stop typing and rewrite certain scenes because they made me feel uncomfortable, I knew that as a writer who believes in the art of literature, I couldn't. I refused to turn against my own beliefs on behalf of making myself, or others, more comfortable.

Pricey: Playing in Traffic was written exactly as I heard it, saw it, and felt it in my mind. Although this story is a work of fiction, please understand that Billie and Carmine are two deeply damaged characters, and sadly, may mirror the slaves who live amongst us today. They've probably made decisions that the average sane person could never fathom. I would also like to remind the readers that once some people go through things as traumatic as sexual, physical, mental abuse, human trafficking, or any form of human indecency, they most likely will never be the same.

Human trafficking is a very REAL issue. If you or anyone you know is in need of help, please make sure to call the numbers below.

Help lines:

- National Human Trafficking Resource Center:
  (888) 373-7888

- National Runaway Safeline:
  1-800 RUNAWAY (786-2929)

- National Center for Missing & Exploited Children's Cyber Tipline:
  (800) 843-5678

Author Bio

A lover of literature, good music, movies, and art, Fabiola Joseph is multifaceted. She was raised in Silver Spring, Maryland, and while in middle school, she found her passion for reading and writing. She began her love affair with the power of the written word, and it was clear that writing was her destiny.

In 2011, *The Art of Deceit,* a novel about the grime that dwells behind the shadows of hip-hop, through the eyes of a video vixen, was released. In 2012, she coauthored the erotic tale *Porn Stars 1 & 2,* which provided readers with a behind-the-set look into the pornographic lifestyle. November 2012, Fabiola unleashed the fifteen-year-old serial killer Scarlett Rose. *Rebel's Domain* is new and exciting, and brings something different and captivating. Suffocating in darkness, this teenager is nothing like any girl you've ever read about before. Her newest release is *NIYA: Rainbow Dreams*. *NIYA* explores the world of a stud lesbian named Niya and her best friend, Jamilla. This is a story about two young women who are coming to terms with who they are. It's a touching tale of friendship, love, dreams, and murder. *Niya 2: Dreamer's Paradise* was released in 2014, continuing the Niya saga.

Ms. Joseph also published two short stories. "The Bully Bangers" deals with a growing problem in America's schools. "The Bully Bangers" brings justice to the jilted with a twist where the predators become the prey. "Truth or Death" brings readers a new meaning to couple's therapy and the repercussions of a man who is living a double life.

Fabiola is uncompromising when it comes to her work. She believes that for her there is no box, so never try to fit her talents into one. Taking risks, being open and free within the realms of her words, and writing from the heart is the only code she lives by within the domain of literature. Enter her world and she promises that you will not come out the same. With her pen, she plans on changing the world.

*In 2015, Fabiola signed a multi-book deal with Urban Books, LLC. *Niya 1 & 2* will be turned into one book and released 2016. It is no longer available for purchase independently.

Contact Fabiola Joseph:

Twitter:
Soulofawriter

E-mail:
Soulofawriter3@aol.com

Facebook.com/Fabiola.Joseph3

Instagram:
TheArtOfBeingFabie

Web site:
TheArtOfFabiolaJoseph.com

31901061143220